STRANDED &
SEDUCED

SHELLEY MUNRO

MUNRO PRESS

Stranded & Seduced

Print ISBN: 978-1-99-106375-5
Ebook ISBN: 978-0-473-31100-1

Cover: Kim Killion, The Killion Group, Inc.

Munro Press, New Zealand.

First Munro Press electronic publication December 2014
First Munro Press print publication December 2024

DEDICATION

For Paul, my husband, partner in crime, and fellow adventurer.
Every day is a good day. I love you.

INTRODUCTION

Resistance is futile.

Cimmaron Zhaan refuses to follow the traditional path of a Dlog woman. Instead, she dreams of traveling through space and flying spaceships for the Coalition. Years of hard work bring her goal within grasp until her superior seeks sexual favors and leaves her stranded on the isolated planet of Marchant.

Enter sexy club manager Tamaki Grierson. Cimmaron's not looking for a mate, but there's no denying that sparks fly between them. Desperate to leave Marchant, all she wants is to keep her head down and work—no romance for her.

But there's something strange about the club, and curiosity leads

Cimmaron into trouble. Before she knows it, she's naked with Tamaki and his best friend. Kisses. Heated embraces and torrid sex. Their loving is breathtaking. Her resistance is at low ebb, her heart and mind battling her overwhelming attraction for Tamaki. If she isn't careful, her Dlog hormones will tie her to him for life and her struggle to fly spaceships will be for naught.

Warning: This sexy romance contains one ménage a trois scene.

CHAPTER ONE

The bastard had left!

Cimmaron Zhaan stared around the empty transport bay, shock kicking her in the gut. She strode a tight circle to survey her surroundings—just to make sure. Her footsteps resounded in the cavernous spaceport. A droid scooted in front of her, and she snarled under her breath, sidestepping to dodge the worker. Empty. The echo of her boots mocked her, underlining her stupidity in trusting anything the captain said. The *phrullin'* male had taken off early, leaving her stranded with minimal possessions and even fewer credits to her name.

Stranded.

Anger burned through her, and her hands fisted then squeezed as she imagined wringing the captain's beefy neck. The weight of stares from the maintenance crew jerked her from pissed to controlled and inscrutable. Yeah, she'd known the arrogant bastard had expected her to act grateful when he'd suggested they while away the long voyage from Risches to Stavek by sharing a cabin. She'd turned him down flat, and he'd transferred his attentions to one of the lesser crew. But Campbell hadn't forgotten her slight. In fact, he'd gone out of his way to make her life difficult. Leaving her stranded on isolated Marchant was the latest in a long line of Campbell-created annoyances.

Cimmaron stalked past the maintenance men and their droid workers with her nose in the air. Inside, she seethed. What the hell was she gonna do now? Campbell had told her to wear mufti while on leave, so she didn't even have a uniform to prove she was a pilot. All her papers were on the *Intrepid*. She stormed down a long corridor to the communication center, this method of contact the best way to ensure he accepted her call. One hour later, the telecommunications tech put her through to command on the *Intrepid*.

"Ah, Officer Zhaan." Campbell sat at ease in the pilot's chair, his tunic blindingly white while his dark eyes bore a trace of smugness.

Bastard. "Captain Campbell." Cimmaron jammed the tip of her tongue behind her teeth instead of blurting the obscenities she wanted to level at him.

"You were late. We had our allocated time slot to depart."

Cimmaron's eyes narrowed, but she refused to react any further, giving him the leverage to land her in even deeper crap.

"This will go on your record, Officer Zhaan."

Too late. It seemed the situation was already beyond mere apologies and groveling. "You told me we were leaving at second moonrise."

"First moonrise," he countered. "Officer Zhaan, I have noted on

4

your record you are AWOL."

"You lied. You told me second moonrise."

The tinge of red on his prominent brow warned her she should've held her tongue. His pointy ears twitched—a sure sign of impending displeasure. "None of the other crew was late back from leave."

Cimmaron's nails dug into her thighs, and the heat of temper crawled across her cheekbones. *Phrull*, she was probably flashing gold with her emotions, sparkling like the backside of a glow bug—an unfortunate side effect of being a Dlog. "Are you going to come back for me?"

"Return for one female. I don't think so. Officer Zhaan, I'd say you're officially screwed." A smirk formed on his lips, echoing in his sly eyes. "Over and out."

The *phrullin'* bastard. The need to scream swelled inside her. She wanted to punch and kick and exert bodily harm on the slimy male. He might have screwed her chances of flying with the Coalition again, but she'd exact her revenge. One day, when he was least expecting her move. She exited the communications room with precise steps, her back stiff with pride. The five staff manning communications had heard everything. It was obvious by the silence that even now spilled out of the room after her, taunting and full of ridicule.

Desperate to outrun her fears, the panic threatening to overwhelm her, Cimmaron stormed from the spaceport and pushed into the crowd thronging the narrow alleys outside.

Market day. Locals shopped and hustled. Visitors purchased supplies to fill dwindling reserves on their short stopovers between destinations. Traders and hawkers shouted at the tops of their voices, trying to attract customers and extract credits. No doubt thieves trolled the alleyways, looking for the green and unwary who carried purses full of gold for the taking. She had no idea where she was going or what to do.

Blindly, she attempted to control her blooming panic, the knowledge that the captain's petty revenge had left her vulnerable and in big trouble. Her record would reflect the transgression unless she could prove her innocence. She'd have to travel to Coalition headquarters on Bezant. Somehow. It wasn't going to be easy with no currency to pay for her passage. The rumors of space pirates and abductions in this galaxy meant people were wary of giving strangers rides.

Deep in thought, she bumped into a short, blue female, almost knocking her to the ground.

"Sorry," Cimmaron said.

"Hoy, watch it." The female struggled to maintain her footing on the slick cobblestones.

Cimmaron grabbed the female's upper arm, holding her upright when the crush of humanity behind threatened to push her to the cobblestones. "My apologies," she said in a formal tone when the danger was past.

The female righted the white cowl covering her shiny, pale blue head and glanced at the splotches of mud decorating the hem of her robe. "I look like a low-caste." A trace of alarm flickered over her face. "*Phrull*, I need this job."

"Job?"

"They're hiring at the club. I must go. They'll close the doors when they have enough applicants." The female darted through a gap in the crowd before Cimmaron could question her further.

The female's words kept reverberating through her mind. A job. A job. *A job.*

A rumbling sound punctuated her thoughts, and she bolted after the female, elbowing her way through the alley crowded with market goers as she tried to follow. No currency. She would starve, and she had to eat. A job was the solution—the only alternative she had if she wanted to leave this goddess-forsaken planet and exact revenge from that *phrullin'* bastard Campbell.

In desperation, Cimmaron increased her pace, managing to keep the female in sight despite the throng in the marketplace. The woman turned a corner, disappearing from sight. Cimmaron sprinted around the bend in the lane. Where was she? Ah! She caught a flash of white as the female entered a nondescript stone building. With an extra burst of speed, Cimmaron raced toward the building, fear dogging her heels when she noticed the door closing. In desperation, she shoved at it, muscling her way inside even though the bulky Maxiom security guard attempted to slam the door in her face.

"Just a *phrullin'* second. Let me in." Cimmaron kicked his shins, gaining precious inches when he stepped out of range. "I want to come inside."

The door opened a fraction more, and the Maxiom sneered at her, his forehead caste mark glowing and underlining his contempt. Cimmaron stiffened, knowing what he saw—mud-speckled trews and a unisex brown tunic that hid every hint of feminine curves. If she'd worn her uniform, he would have treated her with respect, but his doubt was clear as his gaze traveled down her body and back up again. "You? Behind a bar." His single brow rose halfway up his bald head to emphasize his skepticism.

Phrull, this job was bar work? Crummy bar work. Having her ass pinched, and her breasts grabbed was not Cimmaron's idea of a good time. But it was better than the alternative.

She inhaled, trying to drag life force into her lungs after her sprint through the marketplace. Her chest heaved under her brown tunic, each breath coming with a wheeze.

"Take a number," the security guard said, his tone off-putting as if he thought she was wasting her time. Cimmaron scanned the room, her breath squeezing halfway up her throat in sudden consternation. Maybe she *was* wasting her time. For a start, the rest of the applicants were clean. Well-groomed. She eyed the nearest one, trying to quell her tension. And they were little—compared to her at any rate. Feeling conspicuous, even more than she had earlier, she accepted a white card bearing a number from the security guard and slinked away to find a wall to lean against in the hope of appearing smaller.

In her work as a pilot, she downplayed the natural good looks of the Dlog as much as possible. It made things easier on the job, although it hadn't stopped Campbell from propositioning her and taking enough offense at her refusal to leave her stranded.

Cimmaron scowled, guessing the captain's next move would be to pronounce her transgression officially. Everything she'd worked and strove for ripped from her grasp because one bloody male couldn't keep his gonads under control. She had to get to headquarters first before the *Intrepid* finished its voyage and returned to base.

The rest of the females and the couple of males in the group took a collective breath and straightened. Cimmaron slouched lower against the wall, hoping she wouldn't stick out like pustules on an underling's face.

All for naught.

The man was tall. He prowled into the bar like a sleek *tigoth* beast from the planet Dalcon. His piercing blue eyes scanned the faces in the room, taking his time before his attention rested on her. And lingered.

A frisson of awareness shot through her body and gathered on her lips as she studied his form-fitting black trews and shirt, his matching black boots. Her mouth tingled insistently until she broke down and moistened her lips with her tongue. The expression in the male's eyes intensified, making them darker, more compelling. Finally, *finally*, his gaze moved on, leaving Cimmaron weak and panting. What the *phrull* had that been about?

In confusion, she stared, trying to analyze the sheer need coursing through her body, tugging at places that hadn't seen light for a long time, let alone reacted to a male in this way before.

He was tall, maybe a fraction taller than her. That was unusual in itself. Cimmaron towered above all of her shipmates and only felt at home on her home planet of Risches. His hair was the color of deep space—black. But it didn't hold the nothingness of the uncharted territories. It glowed under the lights, the black-blue sheen making her want to touch it to discover if the locks felt as soft as they appeared.

He turned to speak to the male at his side. Cimmaron hadn't noticed him at first, but she saw he was much the same height. His look was more familiar, that of a local Marchant, which was why he hadn't stood out as much. The deep rumble of the first male's voice tugged at her.

A tremor sped through Cimmaron—unusual and unprecedented, and she wondered what the *phrull* was wrong with her. She was in the worst situation, stranded with no hope of rescue, yet suddenly all she could think about was the male. The need to touch was a siren song in her blood. Her fingers prickled, her lips still tingled, and the rest of her body was...aware.

The male spoke. "I'll see you in number order. Please form a line. Rico will show you into my office when your number is called."

Cimmaron scowled down at her number. Last in, she had the final interview. Knowing her luck, the jobs would be gone by the time they called her number.

The line moved rapidly. They asked some of the applicants to go behind the bar and mix specific drinks. If she managed to get that far, she'd gain a job. Years of saving to purchase her way into the pilot program had made her more than competent behind a bar, not that this looked like a classy joint. The outside appeared uninspiring—a building she'd have walked past if she hadn't been following the blue female. The inside didn't look much better, although it was clean. She'd worked in better and in far worse. Bottles of alcohol from the far reaches of the galaxy lined the wall. The bar gleamed, but it had none of the ornate carvings of some of the clubs and high-class joints. There was a dance floor. Tables. Maybe the place would look better at night when people and music filled the empty spaces. Two spiral staircases led to a mezzanine floor above. What was up there? She craned her neck in her attempt to see. A being standing up there would have a good view of the bar and dance floor. It was probably another bar or maybe private rooms for the rich or those who could afford to pay for privacy.

Time trickled past. Cimmaron fidgeted, trying to ignore the flitting looks she received from the other applicants. Her stomach contracted, and it wasn't just hunger pains. Nerves danced inside her belly as she came closer to the front of the line. Desperation. Maybe. No, not worry. She hadn't felt rattled until she'd seen the male conducting the interviews. The casual line shuffled forward.

"Next!" Cimmaron jerked to attention when the security guard nudged her in the middle of her back. "You. Move it. Don't have all moon cycle for you to dawdle."

Cimmaron turned to glare at the large male. She'd met his like before—lots of roar to scare everyone but not necessarily the guts to back it up when things became tough. Her gaze crawled across his broad face. She could take him with no problem if she wanted. A soft chuckle had her whirling around, lightly balanced on her toes in a defensive stance.

"Come in and take a seat. I'll be back in a couple of *microts*."

The black-haired male held the door open for her then disappeared, leaving her staring after him. His scent—fresh, crisp and green—reminded her of the wide-open savannah country and towering forests on her home planet of Risches. The alluring scent brought a shaft of homesickness. Despair. She'd never see home again unless she managed to get this job. Not that she liked to stay on Risches for too long, not with her stepfather harping on about a female's proper place. Mating and procreation. Not if she had her way. She generally only stayed two or three moon cycles at most. Despite their differences regarding the way a female should act, she did love her mother.

Cimmaron sank onto an upright alloy chair, desperately pushing aside the rising panic and anxiety tangling inside and writhing through her heart. Campbell had not only left her stranded—he'd left her vulnerable. Vulnerable was bad. Vulnerable was a stepfather who hated her and made no secret of the fact while he drove a wedge between her and her mother. A scowl distorted her lips at the thought. She shouldn't have wanted to go home, but she hadn't seen her mother for over twenty moon cycles. Before, she'd had the freedom and luxury of being able to return home when she wanted, on her terms. Now a dark cloud

11

hovered above her head.

AWOL. *Phrull* the captain for leaving her on this isolated planet. A soft click behind made her spine hit the back of the chair.

"So you want to work here." His voice sounded deep. Husky. It sent a shiver of pure longing pulsing through Cimmaron. Her stomach sucked in while blood pooled low with zing-like pleasure. What was wrong with her today?

This male—he wasn't her type. If she wanted a male, she'd look to her own race, not an otherlander. And wanting a male was about as likely as Campbell returning and telling her the stranding was all a bad joke. There was more to life than mating. And so much more than spending life as a slave to a mate.

"Yes, I'm good at my job." True. She was a good pilot. Also, a reasonable bartender.

He nodded, his expression not giving anything away. He glanced through the open door. "Sorry, I'll be back in a few *microts*."

Tamaki made an excuse to leave the office. He had to—a matter of gathering his wits before he did something stupid. Like grabbing the golden woman, forcing her sexy mouth open and shoving his tongue halfway down her throat. Hell, he wanted to do more than that. A bubbling ball of confusion lay beneath the desperate need coursing through his body. In his job as manager of the club, he'd seen lots of beautiful women. He'd spent time with some of them on the upper level, fucking their brains out for mutual pleasure. He'd only dated, never felt the need to have any woman three times.

Twice a date, thrice a mate. Now there was the kicker. He'd never wanted that before because no woman had tempted him. He ambled out to the bar, deep in thought.

"Problem?" Rico asked.

"Yeah." Tamaki jerked his head toward his office. "You could say that."

"You want me to get rid of her?"

"No!" Tamaki's reply was instant. No, he didn't want that. He had rather more sensual plans in mind. First, he'd strip the ugly tunic from her body. The chocolate-brown fabric made her appear sexless. Instinct told him that beneath the brown cloth she bore a pleasing shape. It was the way she held herself, the proud bearing. The flash of vulnerability in her eyes that vanished the instant she noticed anyone was watching her, replaced by a tough, no-nonsense attitude.

Tamaki imagined sliding his hands under her brown tunic, fanning his fingers to measure the width of her waist and slowly moving them up to cup her breasts. He wondered about size. Shape. His palms tingled, and his cock woke abruptly, pushing against the placket of his trews with enough vigor to make Tamaki uncomfortable.

"Earth to Tamaki."

"Huh?"

Rico grinned. "I said, Earth to Tamaki."

Tamaki moved so the glossy hi-tech bar was between him and his friend. "We're on Marchant. Remember? Light years away from the blue planet."

"What's up?" Rico stared at Tamaki before his gaze moved down his body. "Ah. I get it. Wee Willie Winkie is exerting his say in the interview process."

"Get fucked," Tamaki muttered.

"Oh yeah. And I'd sure like that. The *microt* I can talk my way into Marianna's pants I'll be sure to let you know. Hell, I might even take out an ad in the *Marchant Communicator*. Hire a market crier or something. Marianna's surrender would be worth the celebration."

Slightly diverted, Tamaki studied his friend and coworker. Rico had taken one look at Marianna, a local, and declared she was the woman for him. Yet he hadn't been able to talk the female into a date, not within the club or for a casual meeting in the city. Tamaki hadn't understood why Rico wouldn't go with any other female. He glanced toward his office. Suddenly, his friend's reluctance made sense.

"I want her, but I can't fuck the hired help. It's against the rules since the company was sued for the Martian scandal."

"Don't hire her—then the rules won't apply," Rico said. "Go and interview the female and tell her she isn't what you're looking for in a bartender."

"Lie, you mean."

Rico snorted. "Come on, Tamaki. You've done it before."

"Yeah, when I was young and stupid. Lies have a way of coming back to bite you in the arse."

"Hire her then, and keep your hands off. You're the boss."

Tamaki gave a clipped nod and strode back into his office. "Sorry about that. I needed to have a word with my assistant manager. I'm Tamaki Grierson, the club manager."

"Where are you from?"

Tamaki found himself grinning. "Who's conducting this interview here?"

"Sorry, I was curious. I don't recognize your accent. The other male too. He looks like he's from Marchant but his voice gives him away as an otherlander."

"We're from Earth," Tamaki said. "We grew up together on a landmass called New Zealand. We've both worked in several of the nightclubs in this franchise chain."

The woman nodded. "I have visited the blue planet."

Curiosity crept through Tamaki. He wanted to know more about her, but bearing Rico's words in mind, he changed the subject. "Tell me what experience you have. Why should I hire you?"

She looked him straight in the eye, her golden irises surrounded by dark lashes that curled upward in a delicate arch. Her eyes were more elongated than his, reminding him of a cat. Man, he'd sure like to stroke her flesh and make her purr.

Tamaki stalked behind his desk and sat, not wanting her to see his growing erection. Damn, he couldn't get his mind off having sex with this female. And despite knowing he was making a big mistake, he was going to hire her—even if she didn't know a fiery *reeb* from a guardian's kiss cocktail. Letting her walk out of his life would be an even bigger mistake. Aware he was skirting the rules but unwilling to let her leave, he continued the interview.

"I worked as a bartender at the Lingam Towers on the planet Dalcon. I worked there for forty cycles. Once I began my training, I worked evenings and week breaks at the Gallant Dragon on Bezant.

Tamaki was impressed. She'd worked at some high-class joints. She had experience, so at least Rico couldn't call him on that. "Why did you go to part-time? What training did you do?"

"I am a pilot. I work for Coalition Shipping."

Tamaki straightened abruptly. "You're seriously overqualified for working in my club."

Her golden eyes narrowed, emphasizing their shape. Her tongue darted out to dampen her bottom lip. Tamaki followed the move with fascination, lust jolting his cock to even greater prominence.

His gut hollowed. She looked defeated, yet anger pumped off her in waves. There was a story here.

"I had a personality conflict with my superior officer. The ship left while I was in the city. The schedule does not permit them to return for me."

The bastard had left her stranded. Her calm demeanor impressed him. Only the tightness of her body gave her away, and the way she appeared to glow when her emotions heightened. Not a shred of feeling showed in her voice.

"The job is yours if you want it. Can you work tonight?"

Cimmaron let out a slow breath. He'd given her a job. Relief made her giddy and relaxed the tension inside her. "Yes. I can work as many hours as you need me." While she wasn't interested in him romantically, she had to admit, as far as males went, his appearance was pleasing. Careful about such things, she allowed none of her thoughts to show on her face. The last thing she wanted to do was encourage him.

"Good. See Rico about a uniform on the way out. The position is worth two hundred credits per week plus a meal while you're on the job."

Cimmaron nodded. At least if she worked tonight, she'd get a meal. Now all she needed to worry about was finding somewhere to live. "Do you know if there are any rooms to hire around here?"

Tamaki frowned, and Cimmaron watched closely, seeing his scowl disappear magically. He was a beautiful male. He tugged at hungry emotions she hadn't realized she possessed. The thought brought a soft, choked sound.

Her pills.

They were in her cell on the ship, along with the rest of her possessions. *Phrull*, this day just kept getting worse. She didn't want to mate with any male, but without the pills to deaden the urge... Maybe she could find an apothecary. The goddesses must be laughing at her predicament. Her mother had told her she was silly trying to outrun her destiny, all because she wished to travel and command her own starship. Prestige and power before mating and offspring. Cimmaron thought it was a good trade-off. She refused to live the way her mother did, slave to that male—her stepfather.

No, there had to be a way.

"I have a friend who might be able to help with lodging."

Tamaki Grierson scrawled a name on a scrap of parchment and handed it to her.

"I will see you later this eventide. Don't forget to see Rico about your uniform."

Cimmaron stood, heeding the dismissal. She'd push through her problems one by one, the way she always did. She had a job and maybe accommodation. She'd find an apothecary next and take things from there. Even if she had to steal to do it, she'd fight the Dlog female instinct to mate and procreate.

She'd fight for freedom and personal choice.

And she'd win.

CHAPTER TWO

"I'm not wearing this." Cimmaron gestured at the skimpy costume she held in her left hand. It consisted of strips of royal blue fabric. Small strips.

"Don't worry, there's more," Rico said with a chuckle in his voice. He reached into a storage cupboard and drew out a pair of thigh-high boots in the same blue as the strips. "Here you go."

Thigh-high boots. Cimmaron gaped for an instant before her mouth firmed into a scowl. "The boots cover more than the rest." She shook the blue strips and held them up doubtfully. "I'm sure they won't fit."

"The uniform is made from shrinkton fabric. When you put it on, the material will conform to your size to fit perfectly."

Cimmaron glared at the offending boots. No doubt they were the same. "I'll wear my own clothes." Even though the only clothes she owned were those she stood in right now. She'd get by somehow, and it would be better than having her body showcased for all to see. The loss of her pills was going to prove difficult enough as it was without men and women who frequented the bar staring at her, touching her.

Unfortunately, the Dlog people drew attention wherever they went because of their golden skin. Cimmaron shivered as stealthy thoughts of sex and coupling slid into her mind. Tamaki Grierson with his piercing blue eyes, his sexy form tempted her. No! She would *not* allow her Dlog hormones to push her into sex with a stranger. Cimmaron thrust the uniform at Rico's chest. "I can't wear this."

"All the female staff wear this uniform," Rico said. "No uniform, no job." His voice sounded matter of fact, but the threat was inherent in his words and stance. He meant business. If she didn't consent to the uniform, she wouldn't have a job.

Well. Cimmaron's nose and chin lowered as pride took his announcement on board. "If one customer gropes my backside, I'll hit first and ask questions later."

"We have security men to take care of that," Rico said smoothly. "All you need to do is serve drinks."

Cimmaron's chin lifted a fraction. He was laughing at her. "All right," she said in a grudging tone. "What time do I need to be back to start work?"

"At moon wane."

"First or second?" Cimmaron accepted the jute bag he handed her and stuffed the offending uniform inside. She learned by her mistakes.

"First."

With a curt nod, she strode to the door and the Maxiom security guard who stood beside the club entrance. His sneer remained intact when she approached, but Cimmaron noticed he edged away, out of kicking distance.

"See ya later, Hulk." And with a jaunty wave, she opened the door and slipped outside.

The crowds had thinned during her time inside the bar, and the narrow lane was almost empty. The closeness of the buildings made it appear later in the day, the solar light not making a dent on the deep shadows. An elderly Marchant woman limped home with her shopping, her head lowered against the stiff wind.

Cimmaron pulled the slip of parchment Tamaki had given her out of her trews pocket and scanned it with a frown. She should have asked someone at the club for directions before she left.

The crease between her brows deepened as a vision of Tamaki Grierson flitted through her mind, along with the inevitable sexual zing. No way was she going back in there until it was time to start work.

A rusty chuckle made the hair at the back of her neck prickle. Cimmaron's head jerked up, and she froze, aware of the danger she'd blundered into because she hadn't been paying proper attention.

"Hoya, looky at the Dlog *chica*," a gritty voice said. "Whatcha doin' so far from home?"

Damn her distinctive coloring, and damn Tamaki Grierson. He had her so wound up she was probably glowing gold again and making herself even more visible than normal.

The speaker was one of a group of Marchant youths who loitered on the stoop of the neighboring stone building, smoking curve pipes and drinking from frosted flasks. Jostling and nudging each other with their elbows, they appeared harmless enough.

She'd keep walking, as if she knew where she were heading, and ask someone else for directions to the lodging place.

"Where's ya man, Dlog?" The male at the front appeared to be the leader. Cimmaron watched his face. His cloudy white eyes told her he was high on *vroom*, the local liquor. *Phrull*, her day just kept going downhill. She glanced at the others. Their edgy gazes darted up and down the street to check for witnesses.

Cimmaron cursed under her breath and prepared to run if they attempted to jump her. Running was probably the only course of action available. One or two youths alone would have been manageable, but five... She sighed, angry for getting into this position. If only she hadn't been so preoccupied with her woes.

"What's the *chica* doin' alone without her man?" the youth repeated, his smirk revealing a topaz jewel set in one of his front teeth. It glinted in the light of one of the flare-torches illuminating the narrow lane.

A rich kid slumming it. Great. Cimmaron backed away, even though she'd prefer to box the kid's ears.

"If ya don't have a man, maybe I'll take the position." The youth's smirk widened as his gaze strolled up and down her body. He made her feel dirty, and the longing to box his ears grew stronger.

"Heard Dlog women are hot," another youth said. "Wouldn't mind some."

Cimmaron caught a whiff of his breath from where she stood. She backed away a fraction more, continuing to watch the leader's eyes for a hint of his next move.

"Sorry, boys." An arm snaked around her waist. "This one is mine."

Cimmaron tensed until she recognized the voice. Tamaki

Grierson. She cast a quick glance at his impassive face. Oh, just excellent. Her new boss, the one male who actually tempted her, the one who made Cimmaron long to give her body, to indulge her Dlog senses, came to the rescue. Why did it have to be him? She inhaled and instantly regretted her deep breath when his clean, green scent threatened to undermine the rigid control she kept over her Dlog sensuality.

She found herself leaning into his muscular body without even knowing how it happened. And Tamaki, damn his hide, took advantage of her slip. Before she knew it, her back pressed tight to his chest, and she felt the reassuring beat of his heart.

"Maybe not your woman for long. Ya shouldn't let the Dlog wander," the boy said. "Might find someone betta."

His friends sniggered, egging him on, and he strutted closer.

"And you think you're the one to take her from me?"

Leashed danger throbbed in Tamaki's voice, but the youths were too befuddled on *vroom* to take heed.

"Move behind me, out of the way," Tamaki murmured for her hearing only. "It's about time these bullies were taken down. I'm tired of them harassing my female staff." Anger laced his words, and Cimmaron felt the tensing of his muscles, a sleek *tigoth* ready to spring.

Slowly, she edged away, but instead of stepping behind as instructed, she stood at his side. Poised lightly, she watched the youths, waiting for the moment they decided to make their move.

Seconds later, the leader launched himself at Tamaki. His buddies moved in a collective unit, backing up the leader. A mistake. She gave a feral snarl and jumped into the melee, her dander soaring high. Lashing out with her right fist, she took pleasure in the crunch of a flat nose. The roar of pain and vicious cursing brought a grin.

Hand-to-hand combat wasn't something that came naturally to a Dlog female preprogrammed for serving her mate, but she was a pilot, and they were a different breed altogether.

She blocked a punch and kicked the youth's feet from under him. He toppled over, falling into an open drain with a mighty splash.

Tamaki knocked the leader to the ground with a bone-crunching right cross, and the remaining three youths melted into the shadows.

"Can't you follow orders?" he demanded.

"No." Her chin lifted in challenge as she silently disputed his thoughts about the reasons the captain of the *Intrepid* had left her stranded. "Not when I'm perfectly capable of helping. I'm not a helpless Dlog flower." Her indignation climbed as she waited for the typical male reaction.

Tamaki smiled without warning, his teeth a flash of white in his tanned face. The fight had ruffled his dark hair, and Cimmaron experienced an absurd desire to fix it for him. She curled her hands to fists and resisted the urge with all her might.

The leader of the youths stirred with a muffled groan. He spat and his jeweled tooth fell out onto the cobblestones. He grabbed it and rolled to his feet with another groan. "You're gonna be sorry," he snarled before limping off and disappearing into the shadows between two of the stone buildings.

"It occurred to me you wouldn't know your way around the city. I'm going in the direction you want." Tamaki took her arm and arched a brow in silent enquiry.

A shiver sped through her body, converging in her feminine heart. The slow, seductive flush of arousal seeped back to her mind.

Cimmaron swallowed. She was *not* attracted to this man. "Tell me where to go." She tried to shake off his touch. It didn't work. Instead, his lips shaped into a smile of incredible charm, one that made her heart beat even faster.

"It's no trouble," he said.

Sighing, Cimmaron gave in even as she silently disputed his words. The man was trouble wrapped up with charisma and sex appeal. She was in a dilemma, and she knew it.

Cimmaron dressed in the blue strips of uniform with misgiving. The cracked glass in her rented room didn't foster much confidence. The smallest strip covered her breasts but also lifted them until they were prominent and left nothing to the imagination. She now had a cleavage big enough for hands to get lost inside. If they dared try!

The bottom half of the uniform covered her from just below the belly button to mid-thigh, leaving her stomach bare. Then there were the boots. The soft fabric matched the rest of her uniform. A modern material made with shrinkton, it adjusted to the outside temperature so the wearer never became too hot or cold. She sighed and unzipped them, ready to don. They were too big when she put her foot inside, but she zipped them up anyway. They shrunk to fit immediately. She peered into the looking glass, studying the reflection with misgiving. With her golden blonde hair tumbling loose around her shoulders and the uniform, she looked like a showgirl from the planet Veyga.

She rolled her eyes at the sexy image staring back at her. Her pilot's uniform was much better and far more her. The thought reminded her of everything she'd lost because of her stranding on Marchant. Somehow, she would make the captain regret his hasty decision. But first, she needed currency. This job was the only option she had if she wanted to clear her name at Coalition headquarters.

She scrolled through her mind, trying to think of anyone she knew who might be in this quadrant and able to help with her plight. Janna...no, she'd transferred several cycles ago. Wilbur...no, he was on the *Savior*, a sister ship to the *Intrepid*. She paced to the door and back. Who else? Ah! Lynx and Shiloh, two men she'd met during a very memorable leave several cycles ago. A bar fight cemented friendships. She grinned and picked up her communicator. If their trading route had them nearby, they'd stop by to collect her.

She hit Lynx's number and waited. When there was no reply, she tried Shiloh's communicator. Frowning, she clicked off, noting her battery was low. Strange that neither of the men answered. She'd try them later before her communicator died.

Cimmaron stuffed her communicator in her cleavage, grabbed her room key, exited, and locked up before she navigated the wide stairs leading to the ground floor of the boarding house.

"Ah, Cimmaron. Tamaki asked me to lend you a coat." Lissa, her landlady, swept from her ground floor receiving room, her pale green robes fluttering around her lithe body.

Irritation flared in Cimmaron. There he went again, trying to organize her life. "Thanks, but I don't need—"

"Lordy, luv! You can't go out on the streets looking like that. You'll cause a riot before you make it past the tavern at the end of the road."

The woman—and Tamaki—had a point. "Thank you."

Cimmaron conceded, accepting the long black coat her landlady handed her. She slid her arms into the sleeves and wondered if Tamaki and Lissa had a personal relationship. Likely, she decided, recalling the greeting kiss they'd shared. "Thanks again. I'd better go, or I won't have a job."

"Take care, luv. Make sure you stick to the main roads where there are plenty of security droids. Don't be tempted to take a shortcut. The streets teem with thugs on the lookout for easy pickings."

"Thanks. No, I won't." Cimmaron wanted to screech but managed to keep a friendly smile intact. She wasn't an underling and barely grown, with not a shred of commonsense. A being didn't get past basic pilot training without learning street-smarts.

Cimmaron lifted one hand in farewell and left the boardinghouse, walking briskly down the well-lit lanes. She crossed the road before she reached the tavern, taking the landlady's words to heart. The streets were quiet. A cool wind blew, chasing everyone indoors. It was mainly a residential area, a wealthy area judging by the number of security droids patrolling the streets. She passed a vendor with a smoked capon trolley. The delicious scents of the capon roasting over hot coals made her mouth water. She had to force herself to keep moving when hunger pangs started.

A flash of movement in her peripheral vision made her whirl in that direction. A being slinked into the shadows. The cowl and robe hid his or her identity. She stared at the gloomy dark until a droid urged her on. Aware she'd be late if she didn't hurry, Cimmaron increased her speed. On arrival at the club, she rapped on the front door. The door cracked open. St. Bridget's ears. How did the customers manage to enter the club with the door firmly shut?

"It's you," Hulk said, moving aside to let her inside.

"In the flesh."

Hulk jerked his head in the direction of the bar. "Rico is waiting at the corner of the bar for the new staff."

Cimmaron stalked past him and headed in the direction he'd indicated. The club looked very different when it was full. Loud music pulsed through the large room. Strobe lights flickered, flashing across the faces of the dancers. Customers were three deep at the bar, and she couldn't see an empty seat anywhere. Two bartenders served behind the bar, both females, and they wore uniforms identical to hers. They didn't seem worried about the brevity of the outfit, but Cimmaron felt her naked belly and shoulders rubbing against the fabric of the coat her landlady had lent her.

One of the bartenders stacked dirty goblets inside a cleanser unit while the other served a group of giggly females. Their pale coloring pegged them as Marchant, but their outfits, made of shiny black leather, were pure high galaxy fashion instead of traditional full-length robes. They'd changed their hair color from black and looked like a bunch of vibrant flowers. She pushed her way through the crowds, finally spotting Rico seated at the very far end of the bar.

Rico slid off his chrome barstool the moment he saw her. "Good, you're here. I wasn't sure you'd show."

"I said I would," Cimmaron said, her tone sharp. Talk about a character assassination. He hadn't even given her a chance.

Rico ignored her flash of irritation. "There's a small room out the back where the staff keep their belongings. You can leave the coat there. I need you to come through to my office to sort out the formalities."

Cimmaron frowned. "What formalities?"

"We program all the employee fingerprints into our computerized system. That gives you access to the stock plus entrance through the main door into the club without waiting for security to answer."

Cimmaron followed Rico into a small office that was only big enough for the desk and two chairs. Parchments and ledgers covered the desk. Rico shoved them aside and pulled a glass disc out of the desk drawer.

"Place your right finger on the middle of the disc." Once Cimmaron complied, Rico flipped over a lid so it enclosed her finger. He tapped a sequence onto a keyboard and pressed a button. The glass glowed bright red. A flash of heat zapped her finger, and a *microt* later the color faded along with the heat. Rico opened the glass lid, and Cimmaron slid her finger free. "You'll see wall scanners next to the stockroom and the bar entrance. Hold your finger up to the scanner, and the door will open."

She nodded.

"I'll take you behind the bar. Give you a quick tour."

Rico showed her where the various drinks were kept, where the chillers, the ice and goblets were stored, how to account for each sale, and introduced her to the other bartenders—Zara, a busty Pinkton with a head full of pink braids, and Melad, a petite bald Marse with tribal patterns covering half her face—before leaving her to it.

Cimmaron left her coat and communicator in the staffroom. Once working, she slotted into her job behind the bar as if she'd always been there. One bar was much like another. She served steaming blue mercury cocktails along with flasks of *vroom*, and the hours flashed past. A purple haze of smoke drifted lazily toward the ceiling from the long, fat cigars many of the customers smoked. Chances to chat with the other bartenders were few since customers lined up at the bar, and the drink waitresses kept her busy with orders.

"Hey, babe. Three *vroom*s over here." The speaker was young and well-dressed in a slick silver suit. Another local.

Cimmaron leaned over to pull three *vroom*s from the chiller.

"Nice ass, babe." He reached over the bar to grab her breast when she turned back with the drinks. Cimmaron was too quick for him and his hand brushed against her bare belly instead. His two friends sniggered, their highly scented perfumes making her nose tickle with the need to sneeze.

"Hands off," she said, maintaining a pleasant tone despite her irritation. Typical chat-up lines. They had to flex their muscles, especially in front of their friends. "I'm here to serve drinks, not offer entertainment."

His friends sniggered again.

His dark brows bristled above his slanted eyes. "But you're a Dlog."

"So?" Cimmaron knew what he was implying but waited for the usual crude comments about Dlog women and how easy they were.

"Do you have a male?" His pale eyes regarded her calmly, but the pinkish tips of his ears betrayed his discomfiture at his friend's teasing reactions.

"Yes, I have a mate," Cimmaron stated bluntly, immediately thinking of Tamaki. She quickly erased his visage from her mind to concentrate on selling her words to the customer. A lie of course, but if word spread about her being unmated, she'd never

29

get rid of the lines of males wanting an easy lay. The rumors weren't strictly true about them being free with their favors since their genetic makeup propelled them to mate. Usually, they mated within their own race, but they could mate with otherlanders just as effortlessly. She snorted. There was nothing easy about having a mate, especially a Dlog one, since they tended to be dominant. Hell, she snarled silently. Why dress it up with niceties? Dlog males were bullies.

Cimmaron added shaved icicles to a silver container, secured the lid, and pressed the mix button. That was why she'd decided to train as a pilot— Shit, her pills! She hadn't found a medicine man to replace her pills. *Phrull.* Appalled at her lapse, she cursed under her breath. She'd have to take care of the problem tomorrow. Already she was starting to feel the effects whenever she stepped too close to Tamaki Grierson. The mixer finished, but she paused a *microt* longer.

Why wasn't she reacting to her male customers in the same way?

The Marchant youths hadn't raised a blimp on her sexual radar, not like her new boss. She tried to think back to her visit to the blue planet. She couldn't remember having this reaction to Earthmen during the layover there. Cimmaron handed the smoking cocktail to her customer.

During her last leave, she'd met with Lynx Leandros and Shiloh Tetsu, traders from the House of the Cat on Viros. She hadn't experienced a single blip on her sexual radar during their encounter, and they were both handsome and virile males. Just three friends having fun, so this reaction to Tamaki brought concern.

"Keep the change," he said, extending his hand toward her.

"Thanks." As a test, Cimmaron let their hands brush when she accepted the credits. Nothing. She dropped the tokens into her allocated currency box. Something in her genetic makeup made her susceptible to Tamaki Grierson. There was an obvious solution to the problem. She'd keep away from him—it shouldn't be too difficult.

Cimmaron worked for another two hours, mixing drinks and chatting with customers. The club became increasingly busy, and she noticed most clubbers didn't need to knock for entrance. They appeared to have passes to allow them access. Surely they wouldn't all have their fingerprints added to the club's database? That didn't make sense. There must be some other means of entry for new clubbers. Cynically, she wondered how much they paid for the privilege.

"Cimmaron, you can take a meal break now," Rico called from his seat at the corner of the bar.

She nodded. "Thanks. Where do I go?"

Rico pointed her in the direction of the staffroom. "Order whatever you want from the kitchen. Be back at twenty bells."

Cimmaron was ready for a break. Her feet ached from working in the high-heel boots and hunger made her stomach rumble in protest. She wove through the clubbers, dodging the flailing arms of the dancers, and headed toward one of the spiral staircases that wound up to the second floor. As she reached the base of the stairs, a woman in a tight red gown brushed past her and sashayed up the stairs. Shortly afterward, a Nolan male sauntered up the stairs, eye-catching in his tight leather trews and billowy white shirt. He disappeared into the shadows at the top.

An arm curved around her waist, making her start. "You on a dinner break?" Tamaki asked.

"I wish you wouldn't creep up on me like that." Cimmaron's

heart thudded erratically against her ribs. The warmth from his arm seared the bare flesh at her waist. It was a seductive heat, and she made herself pull away even though what she really wanted was to lean into him and perhaps even rub against his chest. A purr rattled deep in her throat as she stared up at his sexy blue eyes and smelled his exotic scent, the one that reminded her of her home planet. A shaft of longing pierced her before his cocky grin registered. She huffed and drew herself up sharply. *Phrull*, this man kept pushing past her defenses. She *had* to purchase some pills first thing in the morn.

He chuckled, unperturbed by her irritation. "I'm about to get something to eat. I prefer to eat in company."

Cimmaron found herself propelled through an unobtrusive door near the base of the stairs, his arm around her waist yet again. For a male, he was awfully touchy-feely, and she wished he'd stop. To counteract the desires he generated in her, she concentrated on the staffroom.

The room was smallish and connected to the club kitchen via a hatch in the far wall. A rough wooden table sat in the middle of the room, its top littered with a news tablet, a galaxy gossip zine, plus several dirty platters and goblets.

"What would you like to eat? I'm having the special. Buff steak stew, I believe."

"The special is fine." Cimmaron's stomach let out an embarrassing rumble. Just about anything would do right now. She was that hungry. When he turned away to pass on their order, she couldn't help but notice his muscular body. So much for shoving him out of her mind. Her stomach hollowed out and it wasn't hunger for food this time. Every time she saw this man, she wanted to trail her fingers over his skin.

Tamaki placed the order and turned around before she had a chance to rip her gaze from his butt. The male smirked, his dark brows rising. "Like what you see?"

Hell yes, but she wasn't about to admit it to him. Acknowledging her desires was the path to ruin. "Why you don't wear a uniform?"

His brows raised a fraction higher. "You'd like to see more skin?"

"That's not what I meant at all," she said, her tone testy. Any of the flight crew on board the *Intrepid* would have heeded the warning in her voice. Instead, Tamaki Grierson stoked the flames.

"I'm happy to take off my shirt so you can touch me." He closed the distance between them and stopped an arm's length away. She could practically feel her hormones snapping to attention and bit off a curse. It wasn't fair that she should be a slave to her Dlog hormones. Not fair at all.

"I don't do that sort of thing," she stated, crossing her arms across her aching breasts. The rest of her body was communicating readiness to mate as well. Cimmaron knew she wouldn't get much rest tonight, not with her hormones hopping in this frenzied way. "I'm not interested in sex."

Tamaki wanted to prod for more information despite being her boss and despite the non-fraternization rules weighing heavy on his conscience. "Oh shame," he said, positive she didn't mean it. With her sexy curves and golden eyes, she was made for loving. His body tightened at the thought of sexing with Cimmaron. "You must get very bored. What do you do for pleasure?"

Her golden eyes widened momentarily, and her luscious lips pulled to a tight line. Yeah, that had prodded her all right. Her eyes flashed amber warning lights while her skin took on a stunning golden glow. It made him wonder what she'd look like during the sexual act. Would she glow a more intense gold, and would the color spread across her entire body? The need to know was starting to consume him, and yet he'd only met her.

"I have my job."

But she didn't anymore because her captain had ripped her security blanket from under her feet. "Why do you want to be a pilot? It's not usual for a Dlog female."

Cimmaron's laugh held bitterness and raised many questions. "I don't want to be trapped with a mate for the rest of my life. I don't want to be like my mother."

There was a story there, but he wanted her to relax before she returned to work behind the bar. If she stalked out there with her golden glow, every male in the club would want to try their luck. The thought didn't please him at all. Despite his reassurances to Rico, he could admit his desire to himself. He wanted her so bad he was tempted to drag her up the circular stairs to the level above where mates were chosen and loved three times to cement the irrevocable bond. But even more, he wanted to touch, to glide his fingers across her golden curves.

The need to kiss her pouty lips registered at the same moment he reached for her. His hands closed around her upper arms, and he pulled her to him, his mouth covering hers before she had a chance to react.

She froze but didn't fight. Encouraged, Tamaki took advantage of her complacency. He nibbled on her lower lip and slipped his tongue inside her mouth the second she opened for him. The female leaned into him with a soft sigh, her breasts flattening against his chest. Funny, he hadn't figured she'd give in to him so easily, but he'd take what she was willing to give. He sank into the kiss, sweeping his tongue inside her mouth to explore. She tasted just as sweet as he'd imagined. Addictive as manuka honey.

His hands slid down her arms and behind her back. Firm, resilient flesh met his touch. His hands lowered to cup her butt, and he drew her closer, fitting their lower bodies together. Her hips rocked, forcing a pained groan from Tamaki.

Without warning, Cimmaron jerked from his grasp. Tamaki let her go, his gaze intent as he waited for a verbal reaction.

"Why did you do that?" Her skin glowed in a stunning shade of gold, but her face remained impassive.

"Haven't you ever done anything because you wanted to?"

Cimmaron frowned, and he wanted to smooth away the wrinkles between her golden eyes. She opened her mouth, shut it again then blurted, "I went to flight school." She thrust back her shoulders in a show of pride, and Tamaki manfully averted his eyes from her bountiful cleavage. Time for that later. "I learned to fly a spaceship," she said. "That's all I've ever wanted to do. I did that because I wanted to soar through the skies and explore the galaxies."

A bell tinkled, signaling their meals were ready. Tamaki crossed to the wall hatch and carried them over to the table. A timely reminder for him, even though the need to kiss her again thrummed through his veins. He sat and waited for her to join him at the table. He shouldn't have kissed her, crossing the line between employer and employee, yet he couldn't find it in himself to be sorry.

CHAPTER THREE

"What's up the stairs?" Cimmaron asked. Anything to avoid thinking of Tamaki and the kiss or the fact she'd like to repeat it soon.

Zara shoved flasks of *vroom* into the chiller, filling the top shelf before she turned to answer. "Private rooms, I guess."

"What sort of private rooms?" Cimmaron frowned in the direction of the stairs. All night, between serving customers, she'd seen males and females of different races going up the stairs. Not as many came down, but she guessed it was early if they were attending private parties.

"Two blooming venuses and a blue mercury." Cimmaron turned to serve the customer while she puzzled about the mystery of the upper floor. She didn't like mysteries. Straight up with no bullshit. That was her preference. She liked to know what was happening in her territory. The club constituted her territory until she saved enough currency to leave Marchant.

She continued to serve customers and dodge wandering hands while she calculated how long it would take her to save sufficient currency. Her stomach turned a nervous flip when she came up with several solar cycles. *Phrull.* She glared at the spiral staircases. It looked as if she'd have plenty of time to solve the mystery.

A Luxor squared his shoulders, the bristly tentacles around his face stirring to attract her attention. "Two *vrooms.* On the ice."

She grabbed two flasks from the chiller and poured them into silver goblets. She added several lumps of violet crackle ice. Immediately, the drinks turned crimson red and simmered with lots of tiny bubbles. She shoved them across the bar at the Luxor male.

"Do you know what's on the next floor?" she asked Melad, the other bartender.

"No idea. I haven't been here much longer than you." Melad tossed her bald head. It should have looked ridiculous but the petite female made the action surprisingly sensual.

Cimmaron shook herself at the thought and bit back a purr. She was starting to see sex everywhere. *Phrull*, she had to find some preventer pills tomorrow and pray to the Goddess that Lynx and Shiloh were close enough to pick her up.

Cimmaron cleared her throat. "Aren't you curious?"

Melad paused and shook her head. "No."

"Well, I am," Cimmaron said.

A hand reached over the bar and cupped her breast before she had a chance to move. "Hoy, six flasks of *vroom.*"

"Take your hand off me."

When he merely laughed and squeezed harder, Cimmaron

slapped his hand. Once free of his slimy touch, she backhanded him hard enough to snap his head back. His arm swept across the bar when he moved, catching the drinks belonging to the group beside him. A blue venetian cocktail splattered across the ritzy white outfit of a plump Trateck female. Her shriek of outrage was high-pitched and endless. It hurt Cimmaron's ears. The next *microt*, all hell broke loose.

Cimmaron stood back and watched with bemusement. The Trateck female sprang at the male with the wandering hands, her face turning a bright yellow. Her ears stiffened, transforming from soft and floppy to sharp weapons. Before she could strike, the Trateck tripped over a stool, knocking over more drinks and upsetting other customers. Fists flew. Chairs crashed to the floor, and tables overturned. The security guards came running as more customers joined the skirmish.

"What happened?" Hulk demanded over his shoulder as he separated two brawling Luxors using brute force.

"He groped me," Cimmaron said, pointing at the culprit.

"So you hit back," Hulk said in disgust. "Why didn't you call security? That's what we're here for." When the Luxors resisted, he knocked their heads together. They crumpled in a heap without making another move.

Two worker droids made soft, whirring sounds as they restored order, picking up chairs, broken goblets and flasks, and righting tables.

Hulk stood back, his arms folded across his chest as he watched. With order reinstated, he turned to Cimmaron with a sneer. "If you do that again, you're out."

Cimmaron lifted her hand to her forehead in a snappy salute. "Yes, sir." She scowled at his back when he strode away to do more security guard-type things. She served a waiting Marchant female and her tipsy companions.

"Cimmaron, two *reebs* for my friends here," Rico said, indicating the dark-skinned male and female standing at his side. They bore tattoos on their faces, the scarring white against the darkness of their skin. Cimmaron wasn't sure what planet they hailed from, but they were attractive specimens. She grabbed the bottles of amber-colored *reeb* from the back of the chiller, popped the lids, and handed them over. "Would you like goblets?"

"There are goblets in the room," Rico inserted smoothly. "If you require anything else, use the bar on the next level."

The male nodded abruptly.

Cimmaron frowned. They were going upstairs? She scrutinized them carefully. They were obviously a couple. She sensed the current of awareness zapping between them, and her acute senses picked up the musky scent of arousal.

The male carried the two bottles of *reeb* and ushered the female through the crowd of clubbers. Cimmaron watched as they climbed the spiral stairs. At the top, she caught a flash of a security guard before everyone disappeared from sight.

"What's upstairs?" she asked Rico.

"Customer is waiting," he said, indicating the Luxor at the bar and ignoring her question.

Frustration curled through her, mixing with the slow burn of arousal. *Phrull!* Cimmaron took the customer's order and served several others—male and female from many different planets. She was the only Dlog, but then that was to be expected.

A sliver of loneliness mixed with the lump of tension in the pit of her stomach. Her hand trembled slightly when she reached for a flask of *vroom*. She curled her hand into a fist, then slowly uncurled her fingers, exhaling with relief when the shaking didn't reoccur. *Phrull*, she had to buy pills somehow or steal them as a last resort. Her sense of smell was becoming more acute. The sexual musk in the air was playing hell with her libido, and the tremors had commenced. Add Tamaki Grierson into the mix, and she was in big trouble.

"The new barmaid was asking questions about upstairs." Clear disapproval shaded Rico's words, and he underlined it with a scowl.

"She's good behind the bar," Tamaki said. "The customers seem to like her." It was true.

"When they're not trying to grab her tits. The security guards had to step in when she hit a Luxor male and created an all-out brawl."

Tamaki chuckled. "She's feisty."

Rico sighed. "Remember the rules against involvement with the staff."

"I'm not involved with her," Tamaki said, but once again, honesty made him admit he'd like to have an up close and personal relationship with the golden woman. "Besides, she doesn't have clearance to the rooms upstairs. She won't get up there without being turned back by security."

"Perhaps I should remind her she's here to serve drinks. That's what she's paid for," Rico said.

"Give her a break. You're pissed because Marianna is ignoring you. You need—"

"Don't say it," Rico snapped.

"Sorry." Tamaki patted his friend's shoulder in a conciliatory manner. He'd never seen Rico tied up in knots like this by a woman before. "Why don't you ask her out?"

Rico's shoulders slumped. "She said no."

"Did she give a reason?"

"She didn't want to harm her good reputation by being seen with me."

Tamaki couldn't prevent a snort. The administrative council of Marchant didn't mind taking their rental or the increased currency the club brought to the planet in the way of taxes. Previously, Marchant had been a trading planet where travelers stayed overnight at most before moving on. The club gates brought new travelers to the planet. Tourists. "Maybe you should give up on her? There are plenty of other females."

"I don't want another female." Rico nailed him with a stormy glare. "Just like you aren't going to *phrullin'* listen to me about the Dlog female. You know you're going to have her despite the club rules."

"No." Tamaki shook his head, enforcing his words, but *phrull*, he was tempted.

It was late morn by the time Cimmaron wandered downstairs to break her fast. Tamaki had thought she would never appear. He chatted with Lissa while he waited for her, enjoying his visit even though he was eager to see Cimmaron.

Tamaki caught a glimpse of her when she paused at the base of the stairs to press a hand to her stomach. Her communicator buzzed.

"Yes." She paused to listen. "Lynx and Shiloh? No, I haven't seen them since we met for drinks during my last leave. I tried to contact them last night, but neither of them answered. I don't know where they are." She paused. "Yes, I'll tell them to contact home if I hear from them." With a gusty sigh, she disconnected the call and slid the communicator into her pocket. Her chest rose and fell again before she made her way to the refreshment area.

"Ah, Cimmaron. You have risen from your rest. You have a visitor."

"But I don't know anyone here." Cimmaron entered Lissa's receiving room, stopping just inside the door.

"Good morn, Cimmaron," he said.

"You."

Tamaki wanted to laugh at the dismay on her face. If anyone should worry about his visit, it should be him. He was breaking every single one of his personal rules along with the club rules by being here, yet he couldn't seem to help his interest. He'd woken this morn with Cimmaron on his mind. He'd even come up with a decent excuse for visiting. Yep, no doubt about it. He had a bad thing for the Dlog female.

"What are you doing here?" She didn't move from her spot just inside the doorway.

They both ignored Lissa's gasp of shock at Cimmaron's bluntness.

"It occurred to me you might need an advance on your wages," he said, trotting out his excuse without pause. He could lie with the best of them.

She swallowed, appearing distinctly nervous, even though she had no reason. "Okay. Thanks." She glanced at Lissa before casting another uneasy look at him. "Can you tell me where the nearest apothecary is located?"

"Are you ill?" Concern filled him. She didn't seem weak or display any symptoms he could construe as illness.

"I... No, I'm not ill," she said.

So why did she need an apothecary?

"There's one quite near the spaceport in one of the lanes. It's not a particularly good area." Lissa's brows drew together in doubt.

"I know where it is. I'll escort her."

"That would set my mind at rest," Lissa said. "Would you like some Marchant ale, luv? The servant is making a batch for us now."

"I don't require an escort."

"I promise not to bite," Tamaki said. "Lissa will vouch for me." He didn't bite this early in the morn. His gaze drifted across her face and wandered lower to skirt her breasts. Damn, but he could change his normal practices. The uniform she'd worn at work had given him a fair idea of the areas he'd like to nibble first.

Lissa shot him a reproving look. "Tamaki, really."

His grin widened. "I forgot you read minds for an instant."

Lissa gave a haughty sniff. "Believe me, I'm trying to block *your* thoughts."

"Can you read mine?" That was clear horror on Cimmaron's beautiful face, making Tamaki wonder at the secrets she harbored. There was something...big. Had she told the truth about her stranding? Tamaki dredged up her explanation and shook his head. No, she'd been so indignant and visibly upset during the job interview. There must be something else.

"I haven't tried to read your mind, luv," Lissa said with quiet dignity. "For one, it would be very rude, and secondly, I never read a being's mind without permission. Tamaki's thoughts were so strong they battered down my guards. It *won't* happen again."

The servant arrived with a tray of ale. The spicy scent was rich and intoxicating, reminding him of the mulled wine his mother used to make during the middle of an Earth winter. The servant set the tray on a low metal table and silently padded from the receiving room. Lissa poured the steaming ale into three jeweled goblets.

Tamaki leaned back on the padded divan and idly scanned the hangings on the walls. Because they were old, the colors had faded, but they told an interesting story of Marchant's history and the battles fought to gain freedom from the Orkane.

"Luv, take a seat beside Tamaki," Lissa said.

Tamaki purposely kept his gaze on his surroundings and the images of mountains and lakes etched into the doors of a tall chest sitting against the nearest wall.

He heard the squeak of Cimmaron's boots on the hardboard floor, the confident footsteps as she crossed the room to sit beside him. She claimed the far corner of the divan, sitting as far from him as possible. That wouldn't last for long. Like many of the items in Lissa's reception room, it was old. The roll-together factor would have them sitting closely and probably touching in no time. Tamaki stretched, raising his hands above his head in an indolent move. When he resettled, they were much closer. He could smell her—an attractive scent not unlike the sea on a fresh day. His cock drew up, tightening beneath his trews. Last night's kiss hadn't been nearly enough. To hell with Rico's objections about fraternization and to hell with the club rules. Something propelled him onward. Cimmaron hadn't objected to his kiss last night, and if she continued to be of the same mind, he was going to make his move.

She inched back toward the end of the divan, but Tamaki wasn't having that. He stood to accept a goblet from Lissa and handed it to Cimmaron. With both hands holding the goblet, she'd end up toward the middle of the divan. Grinning inwardly, Tamaki took a second goblet and sat beside her again. Their shoulders brushed, as did their hips and thighs. A gust of air whooshed from between her lips. She shivered, a full-body tremor that jiggled her breasts and made him want to groan. He didn't know what it was about this female, but he had never been with anyone who turned him on so quickly with a look, a soft touch and scent.

Tamaki cleared his throat. "Do you like the ale?"

"It's very good." Cimmaron's voice emerged as a low, sexy drawl.

He glanced up, intercepting Lissa's look of worry. It made him wonder if she'd told the truth about reading Cimmaron's mind. The older woman had an insatiable curiosity when it came to her lodgers. He and Rico had stayed with Lissa when they'd been setting up the club.

Cimmaron rubbed against him, letting out a soft purr. "I've never tasted hot ale before."

Tamaki frowned when she brushed against him again. He didn't want her drunk! He wanted a lover who was fully conscious and taking part because she wanted to spend time with him.

"Perhaps you should take Cimmaron to the apothecary now." Lissa stood. "She doesn't appear well."

Tamaki wouldn't go as far as to say that. Her skin shone in the golden hues he found extremely attractive, and she was touching him willingly. She actually seemed to be enjoying it too.

Cimmaron heard herself panting like a canine and knew she had to get to an apothecary *now*. "Which way do I go?" She stood and forced the words out with difficulty. They came out in a slur. Her body swayed. It was hard to concentrate when all she wanted to do was undulate against Tamaki's hard body and purr like a feline.

"I'll take you." Tamaki touched her arm, and it felt as if she'd received a shot from a ray gun. The current simmered inside her body, jolting nerve endings that were already wired and ready for action. Her nipples rubbed against her bindings, intensifying the reaction in her sensitized body. Cimmaron forced her legs to move and almost groaned aloud at the exquisite sensation of fabric rubbing against her moist flesh.

"Hurry," she pleaded, desperate to get to an apothecary before she attempted to jump Tamaki. Why him? Why now, after all she'd been through to escape her heritage? She wanted to cry yet knew weeping wouldn't help one bit.

"Don't let any other male near her. Stay with her. Don't even leave her alone with the apothecary. Promise me," Lissa demanded of Tamaki.

Cimmaron fought the hormonal surge inside her body, silently cursing the captain of the *Intrepid* and every other male of her acquaintance, including Lynx and Shiloh. It wasn't *phrullin'* fair she should crave a male's touch so badly when all she wanted was to do her job and pilot ships.

Tamaki supported her weight the entire trip to the apothecary, helping her negotiate the pedestrians thronging the marketplace while she fought the demons inside her mind. Her breasts ached, and each step was pure torture. Tamaki wrapped his arm around her waist, pressing her to his side. Her lips grazed the warm skin in the V of his black shirt, his green, spicy scent sending a series of shockwaves skipping through her body. He never hesitated, propelling her along, guiding her down one narrow lane after another.

Heat engulfed her body, and beads of sweat formed on her

forehead. Images of two naked bodies writhing together formed in her mind.

Tamaki. Her.

A loud purr erupted, and the heat in her body intensified. Her entire body tingled on the cusp of orgasm. Suddenly, she didn't care about pills, about captaining a ship of her own or maintaining her independence. All she cared about was ripping off her clothes and forcing Tamaki to thrust his cock deep inside her pussy.

CHAPTER FOUR

Tamaki had no idea what ailed her, but protectiveness surged through him. He needed to keep her safe. She kept rubbing against him and purring like a cat. Normally, he'd enjoy the closeness and work on taking it further, but something was obviously wrong. Hopefully, the apothecary would know the cause and have a cure. Tamaki half carried her down the lane and shouldered his way into the shop.

The area was so crowded with stock there wasn't enough room inside for more than two beings. Jars of mystery items lined the walls. Layers of dust covered every surface, giving the shop a musty, unloved appearance. It didn't smell much better, reminding him of the stench of tomcat's piss.

"Hello?" Tamaki hoped Lissa knew what she was doing sending them here.

Scuffling came from another room out the back. The sound drew nearer until a stooped male dressed in a khaki green robe shuffled behind the battered counter. "Canna help ya?" He slurred his words together, sounding rusty as if he didn't speak very often.

Here, Tamaki was at a loss. He didn't know what was wrong with Cimmaron. A quick glance confirmed she wasn't in any condition to answer a series of questions. Perhaps if he described her symptoms. "She seems hot and keeps rubbing against me. She's purring like a cat."

The male shuffled from behind the counter and peered closely at Cimmaron. He poked her golden arm with one forefinger. "Dlog."

"Yes, she's a Dlog."

The male limped over to a pile of jars and unerringly picked up one from the dozens. He shook it before tugging off the lid. A grunt emerged. "Six left." He limped back to Tamaki. "Pay first."

"How much?"

"One thousand credits."

"One—"

"Take or leave," the male said.

Cimmaron shuddered before rubbing her full breasts across his chest. A soft flush highlighted her cheeks, and when she opened her eyes, they were pure gold. "Kiss me," she purred.

Oh, he wanted to, but there was something wrong with this picture. "What's wrong with her?"

"Dlog female must mate. Go on heat. Pills stop."

Tamaki studied Cimmaron in a new light. She lay weak and compliant in his arms, quite unlike the female who'd strutted into his bar with real attitude and took no-nonsense from anyone. The golden glow was the flush of sexual arousal, not a fever or illness. "Are the rumors true? If a Dlog female has sex with a male, they're mated for life?"

"True, if they in heat. If they not take pills."

"How long will the pills last?"

"One pill last for a par cycle."

About a week, Tamaki translated. And the male had six pills. "Can you get more?"

"Expensive."

Anger exploded in Tamaki and it must have shown. The male took two hasty steps backward, putting distance between them.

"Hard to get," he said, panic on his wizened face. "No Dlog live on Marchant. Must wait for traders to come."

Tamaki took a deep breath, finally understanding the truth behind the apothecary's words. "I'll take all six. Can she take one now?"

"Take awhile to work."

Tamaki gazed at the female in his arms. She rubbed her cheek against his chest, a lusty purr vibrating through her. If she kept rubbing against him in that manner, he wouldn't be responsible for his reactions. She repeated the move, sliding against his groin. His cock reacted to her sinuous stroking, filling and pushing against his trews. Tamaki gritted his teeth and attempted to hold her away from his body. She fought him, stronger than normal in her determination to mate.

"Hot. So hot," she said, tearing at her tunic.

Tamaki struggled to prevent her from removing her clothes. "Does she need to swallow the pill whole?"

The male nodded. "With liquid. I get." He disappeared through the concealed doorway. At least the male was acting with good sense now that he'd garnered a sale. He was letting Cimmaron take one before they completed their transaction.

Cimmaron stopped trying to take off her clothes, and Tamaki relaxed. Mistake. She attacked his self-restraint, brushing her lips across his throat and rubbing against his groin. Tamaki groaned at the sensation that washed through him, the tightening of his balls and cock. He found himself clutching her to his chest and rubbing back. She moaned, lifting her head and offering her mouth for him to take. Tamaki took what she offered before his brain had a chance to kick in. Their lips slid together. Tamaki's mouth opened in shock and her tongue slipped inside, stroking the softness of his inner cheek and contrasting hardness of his teeth.

He shivered, knowing he needed to stop her before they did something they'd both regret yet contrarily wanting to hold her for a bit longer.

The elderly apothecary appeared without warning and slammed a goblet on the scarred wooden counter. "Liquid." The water splashed over the edge and several droplets ran over the metal to pool on the counter surface. The man fumbled with the glass jar and finally pulled out a single black pill. He extended his hand with the pill sitting in his palm.

Tamaki wrenched himself free of Cimmaron. He pressed the pill to her lips and handed her the goblet of liquid. "Swallow," he ordered in a stern voice.

Cimmaron turned her head. "Don't wanna."

"Do it." Tamaki felt the urge to shake her. He was trying to help. She didn't want to mate with him, and although he craved her body, her attention, winning this way wasn't right. He needed her fully conscious of her actions and making love to him because she wanted him. *Him*. Not just a handy cock to scratch an itch.

"Kiss me," she pleaded in a throaty voice, turning her shimmering gaze on him.

"After you take the pill." They stared at each other, neither willing to budge first.

"Kiss me." She trailed her fingers across his face, caressing his cheek and tracing the outline of his lips.

His heart thumped so loudly, Tamaki was sure she'd hear and realize how close he was to losing control and giving in to the urgent desire thrumming through his body. God, he wanted her so bad his hands were trembling. Inhaling deep, he offered her the pill again. "Swallow the pill, and I'll kiss you." Yeah, blackmail, but he couldn't take much more. She had to take the pill. She just had to before he cracked and crossed boundaries he couldn't reinstate.

Cimmaron lifted her tunic to expose the tapes binding her breasts. "I swallow, and you'll kiss me here." She pointed to a rigid nipple beneath her tunic.

Tamaki gulped. "Okay." The word came out with a hint of croak. He swallowed again and hoped like hell that she didn't have any additional stipulations. He didn't think he could take much more.

"Deal," Cimmaron said. "Give me the pill."

He handed it over, still not convinced she wasn't going to chuck it away and jump him instead. In fact, half of him willed her to do just that. Hell of a way to go.

She popped the black disc into her mouth and took the goblet he gave her with a trembling hand. She raised it to her mouth and tipped back her head. As he watched, she swallowed. His breath eased out in relief. Now all he had to do was wait until the pill took effect.

Cimmaron drank every drop of liquid before she slapped the goblet on the counter. "You have to kiss me now," she said.

"We'll need privacy." Okay, that was a good excuse.

"You owe me a kiss. You have to pay. You. Have. To." She punctuated each word by poking a forefinger in his chest. Her cat's eyes flashed a light amber color, but he didn't think it was amber for "prepare to stop".

"Please order more pills." Tamaki pulled a calling card from his pocket and handed it to the elder male along with several currency discs. He received the bottle of pills in exchange and slipped it into his inside jacket pocket. "Call me when they come in."

"Kiss. Kiss." Cimmaron leaned close and puckered up.

"Pills make sleepy," the apothecary said. His gaze skimmed over them both before he shuffled out and disappeared.

Lord, he hoped the pills would make her sleepy soon. "Come on. I'll take you back to the boarding house." He wrapped an arm around her waist and breathed in shallow, careful breaths as he directed her out of the apothecary's shop. She wobbled dangerously when he withdrew his support and almost fell into an open drain. Tamaki grabbed her by the scruff of her tunic and hauled her upright.

"No farther." Cimmaron planted her feet and refused to move.

"Give me strength," he muttered, finally giving up and scooping her off her feet. He walked rapidly toward the club, taking the back streets so they avoided the worst of the market crowds. Just before he reached the club, he turned into a narrow alley. Halfway along, he stopped and let Cimmaron slide down his body and stand on her feet.

She blinked like a sleepy owl. "What's up?"

"You need to sleep."

"Oh. Okay." She continued to stare at him in the same owlish manner before closing one eye in a saucy wink. "After our kiss."

Tamaki cursed silently. Talk about a one-track mind. He

scanned his finger, and the door slid open. He ushered her inside and up a short flight of stairs. At the top, he turned right to his private apartment. Rico lived in the apartment to the left.

Tamaki opened his door, and Cimmaron sashayed, albeit with a wobble, inside.

"Bed, I think," he said, steering her into his bedroom.

"Good idea. We'll go to bed right now." Her smile was wolfish, and if they'd come face-to-face in his club, he'd have worried. Hell, he'd have hidden behind the bar. It didn't take much more than a gentle push to get her on his bed. He tugged off her black combat boots so she'd feel more comfortable. "Ooh, good idea," she cooed. "Let's get naked." That said, she ripped her tunic over her head and loosened her bindings, baring her golden breasts and upper body before he could protest.

Tamaki backed up. "Ah, glad you're comfortable. You should go to sleep now."

"You promised me a kiss."

"All right." Tamaki stalked over to the bed and bent over to kiss her. He aimed for her cheek, but at the last moment, she shifted her head. Their lips collided. Tamaki stilled, his heart doing a high-kicking jig while he stared into her golden eyes. Then her lips moved beneath his, tempting, threatening his wavering resolve to keep things strictly business. Her hands wound around his neck, massaging the back of his skull, drawing him in to her lure. Her breasts rubbed against his shirt, and she moaned, her honeyed scent filling his every breath.

"Feels good. I need more." Her hand burrowed beneath the V of his shirt, her nails digging into his flesh. Her scent tantalized, rich and redolent, reminding him of the warm spices and honey. Tamaki savored her fragrance and the warm, feminine curves filling his arms. Her busy hands scraped across his flat nipple, bringing a shudder of awareness.

"God, Cimmaron. You have to stop."

"But I'm wet for you. I need you inside me. I feel so empty. Please," she whispered. "Please make love to me."

A beautiful woman lying in his arms, pleading for him to make love to her. It should have been a story with a happy conclusion, but he knew he couldn't give in to her demands. Once the pill kicked in and she realized what they'd done, she'd hate him. Tamaki pulled away, disengaging her arms from around his neck and pushing her flat on the bed.

She trembled, wrapping her arms around her naked breasts. "Please, Tamaki. I need you." She spoiled the plea with a wide yawn.

"Sleep, sweetheart. We have plenty of time to make love once you've rested. Okay?"

"I am tired," she conceded. Her eyes fluttered shut.

Tamaki stared, hoping she really had fallen asleep. He waited to make sure and was relieved to hear a tiny snort, a snuffle and then snoring. He gave a tired sigh. Crisis averted.

For the moment.

Five days later

Cimmaron yawned as she cleared off the tables in the club. Most of the customers had left, apart from a few Luxor stragglers. Normally, she wouldn't still be working, but two of their cleaners had run off, declaring themselves in love. Cimmaron made a scoffing sound deep in her throat. She didn't believe in the faithless emotion. There was no such thing as love. Sex, yes. That happened between male and female, but love...

Bah! Males liked to dominate, and she wasn't letting anyone have that power over her.

Tamaki and Rico crossed the dance floor, deep in conversation, and she scowled. Tamaki had helped her purchase pills and hadn't made a move on her despite her vulnerability. Most men would've taken what she'd offered, but he hadn't. She didn't understand why, and her lack of insight whirred her mind into an anxiety soup. She didn't like owing him.

"Hurry up and clean the stairs," Melad said. "Otherwise, it'll be time to come back to work before we're finished."

"Sorry." Cimmaron picked up a broom and dragged her weary body up the spiral staircase.

"What are you doing here?" Hulk, the security guard, demanded.

Cimmaron waved the broom in his face. "Cleaning."

"Hurry up," he snarled back.

Cimmaron shrugged. They'd never been on the best of terms since she'd kicked him in the shins. The male held a mean grudge. Half-heartedly, she started to sweep. Quite a come down from flying a spaceship.

A workman trudged up the stairs, tracking dirt everywhere. His tools clanked against his hip with each step.

"They told me to ask for the security guard," he said.

"I'll get him." Cimmaron grabbed the opportunity to see a little of the forbidden area upstairs. She strutted over to Hulk, her gaze darting left and right. To her total frustration, she couldn't see a thing. Lots of smaller rooms went off the main room. There were privacy guards over the windows, and in the very center of the main room, there was a seating area. Luxurious leather seats sat in cozy groups for clubbers to sit and chat in private. Over to the side, a small bar provided drinks and snacks, judging by the stack of dirty platters.

"What do you want?" Hulk snarled, interrupting her gawking.

"There's a workman here to see you."

"For the alterations. Tell him to come up, and you, get back to work."

Cimmaron cast a curious glance at the cloaked windows before returning to direct the tradesman to Hulk. The curiosity was going to burn her alive until she learned what went on behind the closed windows and doors. She picked up the broom and commenced half-hearted sweeping again, working her way down the stairs.

"Good job," a husky voice said from behind her.

Cimmaron jumped then whirled about, raising the broom as a weapon.

"Steady." Tamaki chuckled and raised his hands in surrender. "It's me. I wanted to know how you were doing. We haven't had a chance to talk."

Because she felt embarrassed about earlier and kept dodging him. She shrugged, giving in to her irritation despite knowing she should feel grateful to him for treating her with such respect.

"I'm fine." Yes, it was abrupt and rude, but she constantly fought the urge to throw herself at him. The sane part of herself knew this couldn't happen. She pictured a spaceship. She dredged up every hurtful comment she'd received about a Dlog female being a pilot. The crap in her past strengthened her resolve to stay the *phrull* away from Tamaki Grierson. But because she wasn't a total bitch, she forced a smile. "Thank you for helping me the other day. I appreciated your help."

Tamaki nodded, his grin strangely absent. "No problem. You almost done here?"

"Yes, I just need to finish the stairs."

Tamaki nodded. "See you on the morrow."

Cimmaron applied her frustration to stair sweeping and finished in no time, her curiosity about the upstairs rooms as strong as ever.

The next moon wane was busy. Galaxy rips had created severe storms that kept spaceships on Marchant for longer than normal and gave the crews some unexpected rest and recreation. Security was busy at the door, turning away uninvited customers while others walked in without a problem since they possessed the special codes necessary for entrance. Cimmaron didn't have time to ask questions, but that didn't mean she didn't have them. Traffic up the stairs during the night was heavy, and even more puzzling was the huge number of clubbers who came down the stairs, ones she hadn't seen before.

A rush of customers prompted Tamaki to jump behind the bar to help serve drinks.

"What is up the stairs?" Cimmaron asked when the rush died down.

"Private rooms," Tamaki said, tapping her on the nose in a teasing manner. She glanced up to see Rico's scowl. The male made it clear he didn't like her, but she was at a loss to understand why. Shoving aside the thought, she returned to a more burning issue. "What sort of private rooms?"

Tamaki tweaked her nose again, and she felt his touch clear to her toes. She was taking the pills, but they didn't seem to work very well in blocking Tamaki's charismatic appeal.

Tamaki smiled at her burning curiosity. "Nothing you need to know about." She was wary around him. Part of him was glad—the sensible part—but try telling that to his body. He walked around with a permanent hard-on these days.

Rico had already clearly expressed his disapproval. Tamaki figured Rico was frustrated because his chosen was playing hard to get. And Tamaki kept reminding himself about the fraternization rules—for all the good it did.

After several moon waxes and wanes, Cimmaron wanted to scream. The need to learn the mysteries of upstairs was killing her. Deep down, she knew it was her frustration at being stuck on Marchant, but that didn't make her need to know any less burning.

She stocked the chiller behind the bar then stomped off to the staff room to have a hot bevee before the club opened for business. The staff room was deserted because the other bar staff had grabbed the opportunity to hit the market for bargains. Since Cimmaron couldn't afford frivolous expenditure, she'd stayed at work.

Restless, she swallowed the last mouthful of the bevee from her goblet and jumped to her feet. She retrieved her communicator, scowled at the low battery readout and tried to contact Lynx. When her call went to message box, she tried Shiloh's number. Nothing. After tossing the communicator back into her locker, she strode back out to the bar. At the base of the spiral stairs, she paused.

Hulk wasn't at his normal post. Before she gave the matter much thought, Cimmaron was sneaking up the stairs, using careful foot placement so they didn't creak. At the top, she halted. No Hulk. She checked left and right, then darted to her left, keeping close to the wall. To her frustration, all the privacy screens were in place. She kept moving until she came to the last room.

The privacy screen was fully open. Cimmaron peered through the glass window. A very large bed filled a good portion of the room. It was low to the ground and covered with a deep green cover so dark it was almost black. On the far wall, she noticed a computer, but she was too far away to see the keyboard. Her fingers itched with the need to explore at closer quarters. After glancing in both directions to see if anyone was watching, Cimmaron crept closer and tried the door. The handle turned at her touch, so after another quick glance up and down the passage, she slipped inside.

Immediately, her heart skipped a beat, her stomach prickled, and worst of all, her nipples pulled to hard nubs.

Tamaki.

She whirled around, expecting to see him standing behind her, but the room was blessedly empty. Slowly, her breath eased out. She inhaled, and the lightheaded sensation eased. She laughed, a low, tinkling sound of apprehension. Guilty conscience. She knew she shouldn't be up here. She walked a slow circuit of the room. It was beautifully decorated, the walls a shimmering green, a lighter color than the bed covering. Beside the glass window, a dark green button shone like a jewel. After a slight hesitation, she pushed it. The privacy screen whirred across the glass windows, hiding her presence from anyone outside.

Cimmaron prowled the perimeter, feeling suddenly edgy and

hot. Her uniform clung to her skin, almost as if the shrinkton fabric had decided she'd lost weight. It chafed her sensitive nipples, and each step she took brought a new wave of heat. She paused in dismay. It felt as if she was coming into heat again. The pills must have been faulty. Tamaki had mentioned the male who ran the apothecary didn't have any more in stock at present. *Phrull*, what the hell was she going to do? For every step forward, it seemed as if she took six backward. At this rate, it wouldn't matter if she managed to save enough money for passage from Marchant because she'd be mated.

The sensual tingle in her nether region intensified, making her long for sex. One male's face sprang to mind, and she muttered a curse under her breath. Tamaki Grierson haunted her dreams as it was, and now he was stalking her waking hours too.

Cimmaron checked out the computer. There were several buttons, but she had no idea what each was for since they didn't bear labels. They were probably for music and to control the lighting. She turned a slow circle to survey the room. It was disappointing really. She had no idea what the big secret was and why this floor was off-limits to staff. Since there was a bed, it was obvious people used the room for sexual liaisons. She spied a drawer built into the wall and pushed the green jeweled button to open it. Yup. The array of sexual aids, ties, and restraints confirmed her theory.

The click of a door behind her made her leap in fright. She whirled about, clapping her hand to her chest.

Caught in the act.

Damn.

"What are you doing here?" Rico demanded, his brown eyes narrowing in dislike.

61

Cimmaron had no idea what she'd done to him, but he made no secret of the fact he didn't like her.

"I'm...ah...cleaning." Pity she'd left the broom in the cleaning cupboard downstairs because it would have backed up her story.

"Right," Rico snapped. "On the bed." He stomped toward her. "Put your hands in front of you." He pushed a button, and chains appeared from a concealed alcove above the bed. Rico grabbed them and, before she had a chance to protest, slapped them around her wrists.

Cimmaron leaped off the bed, but the chains jerked her up short. "Let me go. Now."

"I think not. We don't want our trade secrets blabbed to the competition before we open this room for hire. I told Tamaki you were trouble. Who are you working for?"

"No one," Cimmaron said. "I'm not a spy."

"Yeah, and I bet you can't fly a spaceship either," he said.

There was no mistaking his tone for anything but snide. She drew back her fist and let rip with a good solid punch aimed at his nose. The chains clanked and halted a full range of movement. She missed, jarring her arm instead. It hurt like hell.

"You can't free yourself, so you might as well sit there." Rico wandered over to the drawer she'd opened earlier and drew out a jade green scarf. He turned and smirked at her. "Nice jade green to go with the rest of the room. What do you think?"

"Bugger off."

"Hmmm, that's not very nice."

Phrullin' man was playing with her. Frustrated by her inability to move and her stupidity in allowing him to restrain her in the first place, she glared at him. If he came within kicking range, she was gonna get him. Right in the gonads, she thought with relish.

And she'd enjoy his pain.

He strutted closer, the confident smirk still in play. Bastard.

Cimmaron tensed, ready to lash out, then the strangest thing happened. A shaft of pure sexual need slammed into her, punching every conscious thought from her mind apart from the need to mate. There had to be something wrong with the pills Tamaki had procured for her. They didn't work too well. She was starting to feel like a wind-up toy. Instead of dispersing, the desire thrumming her body grew stronger. She could smell him—or was it because he'd moved even closer. Rico reached out and smoothed a lock of hair from her face, his touch gentle. Soothing. Loverlike.

Phrull! Cimmaron realized she was purring and bit down on her bottom lip. Hard. When she glanced down, she noticed her skin was starting to glow. Funny how gold looked so good with green.

Rico cursed without warning, and Cimmaron jerked her head back, startled. For a long, pregnant moment, they stared at each other. There was a flush high on his cheeks, and his brown eyes were full of heat. She sucked in a hasty breath. Please let him touch her again. Her breasts lifted as she fought to free her hands and touch him. To her relief, Rico cupped her cheek and trailed his fingers across her face again. Smiling, he tied the scarf around her eyes, shrouding her sight. She felt the press of lips against her. It wasn't enough. She needed more. A whimper escaped.

"Please."

Rico let his hand drift lower. Callused fingers brushed across her collarbone then lower, tracing the blue strip of fabric covering her breasts. Her senses heightened by the dark, she waited for his next move. Her nipples hardened to tight points, pressing against the fabric painfully. Cimmaron murmured her acceptance and wished he'd take a more aggressive approach. As if he could read her mind, he bent his head and took one fabric-covered nipple deep into his mouth. The jolt of pleasure was almost too much. Her knees buckled, and she sank back onto the bed. Rico followed and slipped one hand beneath the blue fabric to cup her naked breast. Cimmaron moaned.

Suddenly, Rico's hand jerked from her body.

"*Phrull.*" He jumped away from her as if she were one of the deformed from the planet Lepro. After taking a deep, shuddering breath, he stood, his footsteps sounding hasty as he strode across the artificial wooden floor. A lock turned and connected with a definitive click. The *phrullin'* bastard had left her.

Stranded.

Again.

Tamaki looked up at the sharp knock on his office door. Rico looked downright distraught. His friend's mouth worked but no sound came out. Rico started to pace back and forth in front of Tamaki's desk. He dragged a hand through his hair, leaving it sticking up in tufts. Finally, he dropped onto a chair.

"What's wrong, man? You took terrible."

"I found Cimmaron upstairs in the new room." Rico ran his hand through his hair again, this time in a different direction.

Tamaki smothered a grin. Rico looked like a hedgehog. "It was only a matter of time before she discovered what we do upstairs. She's been like a dog with a bone. I think it keeps her mind off her problems."

"She's a witch," Rico burst out. His gaze slid across Tamaki's face before shooting to his feet.

Alarm surfaced in Tamaki. "Sit. You'd better tell me what's happened."

Rico dropped into one of the seats opposite Tamaki again. "I found her in the room. She was behaving strangely, checking everything out. I think she's a spy for Gynorm Enterprises."

Tamaki picked up a quill and tapped it on a piece of erasable parchment. "Go on." From Rico's agitated manner, he guessed there was more.

"I chained her up." Rico shrugged irritably. "I thought you'd want to talk to her."

"And?"

"I don't know what came over me," Rico confessed, "but all of a sudden I wanted her."

"Wanted her?"

"Stop repeating me, dammit. Sexually! I wanted her sexually." He shook his head, a picture of misery. "I love Marianna. I've no idea why I kissed her. I touched her, dammit. What am I going to do?"

Jealousy seared Tamaki's gut, and he had to force himself to sit still and not react. Rico had kissed Cimmaron. A growl rumbled deep in his throat. His woman. He hadn't been patient all this time to let another man claim her, and especially his best friend. He studied Rico's downcast head. Not that Rico seemed thrilled with the prospect of stealing Cimmaron from under his nose.

Tamaki frowned and tossed ideas around before a plan formed. "Can we do without Cimmaron behind the bar for tonight?"

"Yes, I think so. If it gets busy, one of us can help out."

Tamaki nodded. "I think we should let Cimmaron stew for a while upstairs. We won't open the new room to clubbers until tomorrow and keep it out of bounds for the moment. Are the privacy screens up?"

"Yeah, I locked the door too."

Tamaki nodded. "She won't come to any harm?"

"No. I mean, she's restrained but she can move easily enough and lie on the bed."

"Good. Once the club closes, we'll go and have a chat with Cimmaron Zhaan."

CHAPTER FIVE

Tamaki knew he should have felt guilty—hell, he did feel a little remorse, but Cimmaron deserved this scare. She was gonna be spitting mad when they released her. He looked forward to seeing her, and part of him wanted to experience her anger alone. But he also wanted to see how she reacted to Rico. He hoped it was merely time for her to take another pill, her hormones working overtime to get her to mate, but it was possible she really was attracted to Rico.

Rico stalked into the office. "Everyone's gone. I just locked the door behind the last security man. The travel tubes are on lockdown until tomorrow."

Tamaki added his signature to a supplier contract and rolled the parchment, ready for dispatch. "I'm done." He stood and made for the door. Outside his office, Rico fell into step beside him. They ascended the spiral staircase together and turned left to the newly decked-out room.

"I still think green was a good choice for the color scheme," Tamaki said when they passed the privacy screen.

"I like it." Rico halted outside the door and scanned his finger. The lock disengaged, and he pushed the door open. They stepped inside the room.

Cimmaron lay on the bed, her uniform in disarray and her skin glowing a brilliant gold shade. She must have heard them enter because she turned her head toward the door. She licked her lips and writhed, the motion setting the chains binding her clanking.

"Holy shit." Rico pushed past Tamaki and hurried over to the bed to unlock the chains. They fell to the floor with a metallic rattle. He removed the scarf and leaned over her, his brow creased in concern. His fingers trailed over her forehead before glancing over his shoulder at Tamaki. "What's wrong with her? What have I done?"

"You know she's from Dlog?"

"Yeah. Oh, you mean she's in heat?"

"I think so. She's desperate for a mate."

"Not in heat," Cimmaron panted. "Not."

"But you're burning up. You're glowing more golden than usual." Tamaki touched her forehead too. Pleasure bloomed inside him. He glanced at Rico to see if he'd noticed the reaction and saw Rico was breathing hard. Tamaki grimaced. He knew exactly how his friend felt. It was as if every trace of blood had pooled in his groin. His cock jammed against the placket of his trews, painfully hard. All he wanted was to rid himself of his constricting clothing and feel the fresh life force against his skin, even if it was conditioned and blown through the units.

Through narrowed eyes, he watched Cimmaron rip off the strips of fabric around her chest, letting swollen breasts spring free. At least they didn't need to worry about an unwanted pregnancy because if Cimmaron was accepting both of them, she was right. This wasn't the mating heat. This was something else entirely.

She then knelt on the bed and cupped a breast in each hand. Almost sobbing, she offered herself to him and Rico.

Unable to help himself, Tamaki leaned forward and twirled his tongue around her golden nipple. Jealousy hit him when Rico did the same, but Cimmaron distracted him, stroking their heads, running her fingers through their hair, and encouraging them with her soft whimpers. He suckled her breast, but it wasn't enough. His clothes weighed him down, sexual heat prickling through his body until he thought he might burst out of his skin. Tamaki suspected both Cimmaron and Rico felt the same way.

He pulled away to strip off his clothes, pinching her glistening nipple when she started to protest. Rico ripped off his clothes too, tossing them carelessly on the floor, then as one, they turned back to Cimmaron. They unzipped one thigh-high boot each, casting them aside. The boots thumped when they hit the floor. Rico pulled away the strips of uniform that tangled around her body while Tamaki dealt with the skirt and the brief black panties she wore beneath. Finally, they were all naked.

Such a huge relief.

They toppled onto the mattress in a tangle of limbs. At the back of his mind, Tamaki wondered at the strength of their reactions, but he tossed the thoughts and lingering jealousy aside as unimportant. All he could think of right now was skin-on-skin and touching and tasting.

"Pretty." Cimmaron pressed close, rubbing her body against

both of them and purring loudly as she fingered the family tattoos both had on their right arms. "I like these." The golden glow of her body bathed them, patterning their skin with glints of rich color. Hands stroked breasts, massaged cocks and stroked dappled skin.

"They're our family tattoos. On our planet the tattoos tell of our family histories, our tribe." Tamaki had trouble forcing the explanation out, the thoughts foggy and fading like mist as he gave his body over to the driving urge for sex.

A harsh breath escaped, blending with Cimmaron's lazy purring. It could have come from Rico or it could have come from him. Tamaki wasn't sure. A hand caressed his flanks. Masculine or feminine? He wasn't sure of that either. All he knew was the urgency ripping through him had his hand trembling when he smoothed it over her shapely ass and upper thigh. He followed touch with kissing, moving his lips down her body, licking and nipping at her flesh. Tamaki tugged her legs apart, pushing her flat on her back at the same time. The bed creaked and sheets rustled as Rico and Cimmaron rearranged their bodies. Tamaki leaned over Cimmaron's lower body, nuzzling at her pelvic bone and nipping lightly at the hair-free flesh. The scent of her aroused sex was like a drug that reacted on all of them.

Tamaki kissed and licked the delicate flesh of her inner thighs and glanced up at the same time. The rich rush of desire filled him. Rico winked at him before bending his head to take the swollen tip of her breast deep into his mouth. The sight of her golden flesh and Rico's darker skin made him even hotter. Raw need struck him like a rip wind. Urgency beat at him. He had to touch her intimately. *Had to.*

Giving in to the driving need, Tamaki licked a path the length of her cleft, tasting and lapping up her juices. She mewed, her body writhing under the twin assault of his touch, Rico's touch.

Tamaki's heart battered his ribs, and sweat broke out on his brow. He wanted to stake his claim in a more physical manner. Now. He had to do it *now*. His cock ached, his balls painfully tight and drawn up high and close to his body. He parted her folds, baring her swollen nub to his gaze. Unable to resist, he lowered his head to taste her golden flesh again, massaging her clit with the light sweep of his tongue. Her flavor was wild and spicy, something he could become addicted to so easily.

Tamaki settled in, tasting and teasing and driving himself crazy in the process. He slid one finger inside her pussy. Cimmaron was so wet her flesh parted easily. So he added two more fingers to the mix. A guttural groan sounded, and Tamaki looked up her body. She'd taken Rico's cock deep into her mouth, her cheeks hollowing as she sucked. Rico's head was thrown back, an expression of intense pleasure on his face.

Tamaki's cock bobbed, a tear of pre-come forming on the tip. He fisted his hand around his shaft and pumped once. The friction was exquisite, but he knew it could be even better. Tamaki moved between Cimmaron's legs and guided his cock to the mouth of her pussy.

He thrust slowly, gritting his teeth as her flesh tightened around him, gripping him firmly, sweetly while she stretched to accommodate him. Tamaki kept pushing until he filled her. He shuddered, feeling a ripple clamp down on his cock. He withdrew and plunged deep again, setting up a rhythm designed to drive them both to climax. Not that it would take long. He gritted his teeth, fighting the surge of pleasure shimmering through his balls, just out of reach, so he could enjoy the intense sensations for longer.

"Deeper," Rico growled, his voice thick with passion.

Cimmaron swallowed him down, automatically following instructions. Elation, along with drugging pleasure, shimmered through her body, her breasts, her pussy. She swirled her tongue across the crown of Rico's cock, enjoying the taste of him as much as she loved the full sensation of Tamaki filling her pussy. A purr rumbled deep in her throat. Rico pulled back and thrust inside her mouth again. She squeezed her eyes closed and concentrated on every joyful sensation. The taste, the feel, and the sounds of fucking as the three of them moved together, striving for the magical moment of fulfillment.

The two men moved in counterpoint and increasingly faster. Flesh slapped against flesh. A hand squeezed her breast, and Cimmaron bucked at the exquisite shaft of need that speared her body. Her eyes flickered open just as Rico grasped and massaged her other breast, branding her flesh and causing a corresponding heat in her sex. Desire, liquid and molten washed over her. Her sheath clenched tightly around Tamaki's cock. He thrust deep, stoking the fire burning inside, working his hips like a piston in frantic, almost desperate moves. The fingers grasping her breasts became rougher, Rico's cock harder and his tempo more urgent. It was a wondrous assault, building sensation inside her higher and higher. The golden light surrounding her intensified until she glowed like a star about to turn nova. Tamaki thrust yet again, his cock brushing her engorged clit. She moaned around Rico's cock. Hot spurts of come shot into her mouth just as her body convulsed with the force of her release. She swallowed rapidly, waves of pleasure roaring through her. She was dimly aware of Tamaki spilling his seed, his guttural moan.

Rico pulled from her mouth and settled at her side. Tamaki withdrew and stroked his hand down her body. He kissed her slowly, lingering over the caress, slipping his tongue into her mouth and lazily stroking before pulling away. Rico took his turn, kissing her deeply, exploring her mouth. Tasting her. He pulled away and smiled at her before stretching out and flopping back on the bed. Tenderness welled inside her, and she cuddled up to his side, plastering her damp body next to him.

She glanced over at Tamaki. "Come here," she whispered. "I need to touch you too."

Tamaki trailed a lazy hand over her face as he drew close. He placed tiny kisses, tantalizingly brief across her face then settled so she was sandwiched between the two masculine bodies. Warm and cozy, physical tiredness struck her. Her eyes flickered closed, and she fell asleep with a smile on her face.

A lot later, she woke to hands stroking her body. Masculine voices hummed as fingers lightly circled her breasts and probed her moist folds. A finger teased across her nub and lower, gathering cream. Languid and lazy hands and fingers woke her body, teasing her puckered rosette, sliding across her clit as they rearranged their bodies on the bed. She trembled with sensual awareness, her heart thundering as frissons of excitement poured through her body. A finger probed her anus. Another thrust into her pussy, and the sensation of two fingers pumping into her at the same time sent her soaring high.

Cimmaron kissed a shoulder, caressed a hip. Smooth skin. Masculine skin, and different from hers. Her hands glided across hard muscles, and she followed this up with tasting. She squeezed her eyes closed and concentrated on the sensations simmering through her, the fingers that filled her body with enticing fullness, the brush of a thumb across her swollen bud. Another finger pushed deep into her dark hole, stretching her to the point of pain. She inhaled, savoring the salty tang of sweat, the faint scent of soap, and the musky aroma of sex.

Cimmaron arched her body, sensations piling on top of one another. Her hands wandered lower to grasp the steely hardness of an arousal. She hummed her approval when she felt the pearl of come beaded on the crown. She pumped with slow, even strokes, a guttural groan rewarding her efforts.

The fingers probing her anus pulled out, and she could have howled her disappointment. "Please don't stop," she begged.

A husky chuckle met her demand, and she licked her lips, about to complain again. But to her relief, seconds later, competent hands spread cool lubricant over her rosette. Her stomach muscles quivered while fingers continued to pump lazily deep into her pussy.

"You're very wet," a husky voice murmured near her ear.

Tamaki. Her body softened, and a gush of cream moistened her even further. His thumb glided around the rim of her clitoris, teasing without giving her enough pressure to come.

"More," she whispered hoarsely. Her plea did nothing to ease the teasing. Just when she thought she couldn't bear it for a moment longer, the blunt head of a cock pushed against her rosette. She froze.

"Steady, sweetheart." Tamaki stroked her breasts, teasing her nipples to aching prominence. He bent down to take her into his mouth, his lips closing gently around her nipple. At the same time, the pressure increased as a cock pushed into her. Cimmaron tensed.

"Easy," Tamaki soothed. "This will make you feel really good."

"But it hurts."

"Does this hurt?" Tamaki's fingers smoothed down her body to part her folds and this time he massaged her clit. A shiver racked her body at the same time as the pain intensified. Rico kept the pressure up while Tamaki pushed her higher, stroking in an instinctive rhythm that made the soreness bearable. He stroked her clit, pushing her higher and keeping her at that edge of simmering enjoyment. She gasped as the pleasure took precedence, sucking in an awed breath. Rico pushed past the ring of muscle just as she balanced on the cusp of orgasm, filling her completely, impossibly full.

Before she had a chance to take a breath, Tamaki slipped inside her pussy with a powerful thrust of his body. He moaned low at the back of his throat. She gasped as tiny tremors became bigger. More. Suddenly she shattered, pinpricks of light exploding behind her eyelids, and pleasure swamped her body. Pleasure, so much pleasure.

The men moved together and, enveloped between their bodies, she could feel both of them deep inside her as they thrust, their cocks rubbing against each other. Renewed desire kicked in her belly. Her heart beat impossibly fast. Tamaki pressed close when he thrust. He took her lips in an urgent kiss. Cimmaron gave a small start when his teeth bit down on her bottom lip. The small pain ricocheted through her body until the sensations fizzled and bubbled like heady cacjuice. They overwhelmed her. She felt so full. So on fire. A throaty groan escaped as she shuddered with helpless bliss.

The six-bells alarm jerked Tamaki from a deep sleep. Groggily, he opened his eyes, his head feeling fluffy as if he'd drunk too much *reeb* or *vroom* the evening before. Warmth surrounded him instead of the normal morn chills common to Marchant. He yawned and stretched lazily, snapping to full alertness when his hand landed on warm flesh. A breast. A masculine groan had him jackknifing upward. He stared in consternation at Rico and Cimmaron, his brain pounding in alarm.

Phrull, exactly what had happened the previous evening? He looked at Rico, his best friend, and shuddered. He hadn't? They hadn't? He shook her head, negating the idea even as it formed.

Slowly, images seeped into his brain, and his breath hissed out in relief. A little three-on-three action. Yeah. But he and Rico hadn't done anything more than touch. As he stared in consternation at his friend, Rico's eyes opened.

Rico sat up, his olive complexion turning a distinct green. "Shit, it wasn't a dream."

"No," Tamaki said, trying to stem the renewed jealousy that rippled through him at the idea of anyone but him being intimate with Cimmaron. Last night it hadn't seemed to matter too much, but now...

"What is Marianna going to say? She'll never have me now." Horror laced Rico's words. "And what about the fraternization rule? We'll lose our jobs."

Between them, Cimmaron stirred. Tamaki knew to the *microt* when she realized where she was and remembered the events of the previous night. She scrambled over him and sprang from the bed, her face freezing in an impassive expression. For another *microt*, they all stared at each other.

"What the *phrull* happened to us last night?" she demanded, breaking the taut silence. "I didn't want to mate with either of you, with any male," she said in frustration. "I don't want to spend my life waiting on a male." She raised her arms above her head and flexed her body. The move lifted her breasts, snaring Tamaki's gaze. To his consternation, his cock stirred.

He wanted her. Again.

"I don't feel mated," she murmured. "Maybe it will be all right. I can't conceive if it's not a true mating. Dlog never..." She shrugged, a splotch of dark yellow appearing on her exotic cheekbones. "We don't have multiple partners. I don't think it's possible to bond with two males."

Well, shit. He didn't do multi-partners either, not as a rule, and he knew Rico was of the same persuasion.

"How can it be all right?" Rico demanded tersely. He grabbed up his clothes and shoved his feet into his trews in angry, jerky moves. "I love Marianna."

"You don't have to tell her." Tamaki sure as hell wasn't about to tell anyone about their hot session.

"I believe in honesty in a relationship." Rico refused to meet Tamaki's gaze, and Tamaki couldn't exactly blame him. Waking up in bed with his best friend wasn't exactly a great start to the day.

"There's such a thing as too much honesty," Tamaki said, aware his friend was hurting. Truth to tell, he wasn't exactly happy with the situation. He didn't understand how it had happened. He'd had sex with an employee. Two, if he added Rico to the equation. Tamaki puffed out a frustrated breath. Too late now.

He turned to study Cimmaron.

"Don't look at me like that." Cimmaron scrambled for her clothes. "I refuse to have sex with you again." She eyed his erection with suspicion and backed up a little more, as if he might jump her.

Despite the gravity of the situation, Tamaki wanted to laugh because the idea was at the back of his mind. She studied his body, and the tension in the room ratcheted sharply upward. His cock jerked. Oh yeah, he liked the idea a lot.

"I'm going to see Marianna." Rico stomped out of the room, slamming the door shut after him.

Privacy.

He prowled toward her.

Cimmaron held her scanty uniform in front of her. "Keep away from me." Her eyes narrowed, but he saw the golden glow in her almond-shaped pupils. She wanted him too, and it scared her.

"I'm getting my clothes." Tamaki made sure his face appeared the picture of innocence while he grabbed his clothes off the floor. Reluctantly, he stepped into his trews, maneuvering the fabric carefully over his erection then shrugged into a shirt. He watched Cimmaron all the while, his pulse rate thudding in an erratic manner. Twice a date, thrice a mate...

He was her boss. He needed to keep reiterating the fact to himself because it tempered the need simmering through him to grab. To touch. To sink into her warmth again. Then there was the mating thing. He only ever dated. He never saw a woman a second time let alone the third time needed to cement a relationship.

What most customers didn't realize was that the primary purpose of the club was getting couples together—helping male and female find mates. Life mates. If a couple met once or twice, it counted as a date. If they came together a third time and made love, they were officially mated and bound together for life. Tamaki had never wanted a mate before because of his transient lifestyle. The club managers moved often. It was a way of keeping them fresh and helping the clubs to grow in popularity. Then there was the strict no-fraternization rule.

As far as he knew, none of the managers had mates. He didn't think it was a prerequisite. It just happened that way. Cimmaron moved, interrupting his musing.

"Where are you going?"

"Back to the boarding house. I need to wash and take a pill. Not that they seem to be doing much good."

"I'll check with the apothecary to see if more supplies have arrived. He seemed to think it would take some time."

"I can't afford them," Cimmaron said, her frustration evident from the fisted hands and taut stance. "What are these rooms for?"

"They're for customers who wish for privacy."

"Huh. That's obvious. What else? How do customers get up here? I've seen some walk up the stairs, but not enough to keep business flowing."

"Hmm." Tamaki smiled inwardly. He could tell her, but generally they kept the staff from the downstairs part of the enterprise in the dark. Customers traveled from other planets to Marchant in special time-travel tubes, specifically for the purpose of having a night of pleasure or some to find a mate. Customers came via word of mouth. They didn't need to advertise since Tamaki had the rooms filled every night.

Cimmaron pulled the door open, turning to leave.

"See you later," Tamaki said.

Cimmaron nodded, but fear kicked her in the gut. Whatever had possessed her to have sex? With two men? According to what the matriarchs in the family taught them, it only took one time. A male offered. The female accepted him, the couple did the deed, and they became a couple until death parted them, fertility kicking in at the same time as the bonds. The elders described the mating bonds like invisible chains that clicked into place as soon as the exchange of bodily fluids took place during the sexual act. Of course, those who took the pills didn't have to worry about inconvenient mating because the chemicals halted the process. They were free to take lovers, as she had done on occasion when loneliness assailed her.

Except lately, the pills didn't appear to work effectively, which worried her.

This morn, she didn't feel different. She frowned, purposely striding out with long steps to put distance between them. There were no invisible chains pulling her back to Tamaki. She continued her loose-limbed stride down the passageway, past the other rooms that were still privacy screened and down the spiral staircase. Then another thought occurred. She froze mid-step, almost toppling down the last three stairs in her stunned stupor. Perhaps Rico was her mate?

Cimmaron's heart stalled for a beat. *Phrull* no! They couldn't be mates. Rico didn't like her, and he made no secret of his dislike. It was mutual. Or so she'd thought. Cimmaron scowled, acknowledging the truth as she walked to the door leading to the street outside. She'd enjoyed the sex with both of them last night.

"A threesome." Cimmaron curled her top lip in a show of disgust and grabbed her coat. "A *phrullin'* threesome." What had she been thinking?

After ripping the door open, she stalked through and slammed it shut, taking great satisfaction from the loud crash as it closed.

An elderly beggar, stooped and malformed, limped up to her and held out a battered *vroom* flask that someone had cut in half. Cimmaron indicated the lack of pockets in her uniform, drawing a reluctant grin from the beggar. His front teeth were missing, probably sold to procure currency.

She thought about Rico. She thought about Tamaki. A shiver rippled through her. She'd wanted to walk back to Tamaki and run her hands over his naked chest, explore his family tattoo in detail. And the idea of following the path of her hands with her mouth had occurred soon afterward.

Back at the boarding house, Cimmaron stewed until it was time to return to the club for work. During the walk back, she lectured and told herself it was okay to make mistakes. Mistakes were fine as long as she learned from them. Mistakes were fine as long as she didn't repeat them. She wasn't stupid. Any time she had sex with a male was a risk.

"I will not have sex with that male again. I will not," Cimmaron said as she held her finger up to the scanner outside the club. Despite her fighting words, temptation roiled through her.

"Shouldn't you wait for him to ask first?" a smart-ass called from the front of the line that had formed to enter the club.

"Mind your business," Cimmaron snarled, mortified that someone had caught her talking to herself. She usually exerted more control.

The door opened, and Hulk peered out.

He grunted. "You."

"Yeah," Cimmaron snarled. "Deal with it." She didn't wait for an answer but stormed past him into the club.

After dumping the jacket her landlady had lent her inside the staff room, she headed behind the bar to help set up.

The first person she saw was Tamaki. Her footsteps faltered, and finally, she halted completely. It felt as though someone had punched her hard in the chest. Every particle of life force eased from her lungs, and she gasped, trying desperately to replace it. His scent seemed to swallow her whole, and a spark ignited in her pussy.

Panic roared through her. Stupid Dlog hormones. She quickly calculated when her next pill was due. No, she hadn't missed one. Maybe her stepfather was right, she thought, still in panic mode. Maybe there was no way to control the Dlog genes, no way to outrun her heritage. Maybe Tamaki was her fate.

There were worse ways to go, a traitorous voice whispered through her mind.

She drew a sharp breath and reached for a stack of drink mats ready to set out on the bar. Her hand trembled violently, and she snatched it away, hiding it at her side.

"Cimmaron." His husky voice pushed her traitorous body even harder. Her nipples perked right up, and her stomach hollowed. She wanted to turn around and step right into his arms. Another tremor shook her body as she fought the urge.

"Cimmaron?" He touched her shoulder, and she felt it right to the tips of her toes. They curled upward inside her boots. She was *not* going to succumb to him again. No matter how much she craved his touch. She was strong. She was a pilot, dammit.

"Are you okay?"

She couldn't look at him without giving away how much she wanted him. Like a fire, the need burned inside. "Fine," she muttered, trying to control the shaking of her hands as she started to set up the bar.

"That's good," he said. "Melad has called in sick with Mercury space flu. I'm going to work the bar tonight in her place."

Cimmaron managed a nod of assent. Oh joy. An evening of torture by close association. She only hoped she didn't break down and start drooling, or even worse, lick. No! Worse than that would be if she crash-tackled him and licked while everyone was looking. It would make a great floorshow. She shuddered, wanting to carry out the self-prohibited actions. Desperately. Hell, maybe she would even kiss him as well.

Aware he expected her to speak, she said, "It's good we won't be short-staffed. There was a big line of customers waiting outside. Should be busy tonight."

"Yeah, the space storms are keeping most of the ships grounded."

It seemed as if he might linger and chat, and she tensed at the idea of polite chitchat. She'd never handle nonchalance for long. Her sanity hung by a thread as it was.

"I'll go to the cellar to get some crates of *vroom*." Yes, she was a coward and running away. But it was either that or act on the urgent need to grab him. *Phrull*, what a mess. She forced herself to stomp down to the cellar. If she ever came face-to-face with the captain of the *Intrepid* again, she was gonna thump him through to the next galaxy. This was his fault.

The club opened not long after she finished stocking the shelves. Cimmaron made sure she worked the opposite end of the bar to Tamaki, dispensing drinks efficiently. Grumbles about the space storms were few since it wasn't often crews had leave in Marchant. The bar did a roaring trade. The customers were three and four deep at the bar, the dance floor music loud and the crowd jovial.

"Hey, beautiful. How about a drink down here?"

A pang of envy struck her hard when she saw their uniforms. Space jockeys out for a little recreation. "Sure, won't be long." Cimmaron finished the carousal cocktails she was mixing for the black-skinned Darians before moving toward the pilots.

"Hi, boys. What will it be?"

"I'd like hot sex laced with you," a golden-haired stud said.

Cimmaron shook her head and grinned at the same time. "Not

in this lifetime, but I can get you a drink."

"Can't blame a guy for trying." Blondie leaned close, and Cimmaron sensed rather than saw Tamaki's interest in the conversation. An idea formed. Her smile brightened.

"Drink?"

"Don't mind him. He's a terrible flirt," another of the pilots said.

"Takes all kinds." Cimmaron shrugged, allowing her grin to remain in place. She'd show Tamaki how much the previous night meant to her.

"We'll have two *vroom*, a *reeb* and three blue venetians," Blondie said.

"Coming right up." Cimmaron walked away with an extra sway in her step. The prickling of her skin told her they watched every twitch of her ass with interest. She bent over to grab two bottles of *vroom* and the *reeb* from the chiller. A whistle pierced the air, carrying above the pounding beat of the music. Cimmaron glanced over her shoulder and winked at the pilots before turning back to the task at hand. After placing the flasks on the bar, she made the cocktails and accepted payment with a smile. She moved on to serve the next customer. Another *vroom*. Didn't people realize the stuff rotted their brains?

"What are you doing?" Tamaki asked in an undertone. His warm breath skimmed across her cheek when he leaned close.

Cimmaron tossed her head, putting precious distance between them, and fought the weakness in her knees. "Merely being friendly."

"Didn't look like that to me."

"What? I'm not meant to act pleasantly toward the customers?"

Tamaki cast a quick look toward the group of raucous pilots.

"Not that friendly."

"I work here. As long as I do my job, you have no cause for complaint." She stomped away, her back straight and the hairs at the back of her neck prickling with danger the entire time. Throughout the evening, he kept looking at her. Not that she caught him out, but she sensed his interest. Her body simmered in a state of arousal for the entire session, an annoying prickle rippling across her skin.

"Stop looking at me," she said. Edgy and off-balance, she wanted to lash out with more than words.

"Merely observing your technique," he said smoothly. "I need someone to train the new staff."

"Not me," Cimmaron fired back. Luckily a customer stepped up to the bar, wanting a refill of his *reeb*, so she had a good reason to turn her back on him.

"A Dlog," the customer said. His three eyes looked up and down her body. "Are you mated?"

Tamaki stepped up close. She smelled his clean, green scent before he touched her. His arm slid around her waist as if he had every right.

"Yes, she's mated." He stared at the middle eye of the Usplop until all three of the creature's eyes glanced away.

"Pity. I need company on my ship. Gets lonely traveling from trading post to trading post."

"Maybe you'll find someone upstairs," Tamaki said.

Upstairs? Cimmaron scowled. In between customers, she'd watched the stairs. She hadn't noticed one person going up there. It must be awfully quiet on the upper level. The Usplop wouldn't find a mate on the second floor.

The creature brightened, tiny tentacles stirring at the side of his oblong head. Cimmaron suppressed a shudder. No telling what happened to the creature's body when he was in a state of sexual excitement.

"Take this," Tamaki said, handing the creature a disc. "That will get you past the security guard. If you decide to partake of entertainment upstairs, we'll deduct currency from your account. The hostess will answer any of your questions."

The creature hesitated before giving a decisive nod. The sharp move sent a ripple through his tiny tentacles. "I will partake. It is no good traveling alone." He took the drink Cimmaron handed him and ambled to the stairs. She watched until he disappeared out of sight at the top. Questions trembled on the tip of her tongue, the curiosity almost killing her. Turning to Tamaki, she opened her mouth to ask, only to shut it again when she noticed his arched brows. Silent laughter lurked in his eyes. She whirled away and stalked to the opposite end of the bar, muttering under her breath. "Jerk."

She attempted to keep away from Tamaki, but the infernal man kept brushing past her, the narrow space behind the bar not giving much leeway when it came to passing.

"Quit it," she snapped.

"Just doing my job," he countered.

Yeah right. "It's not as busy now. Why don't you do some paperwork or something equally boss-like?"

Tamaki chuckled. "I'm watching the staff. That's in my job description. What can I get you to drink?" he asked a pilot.

Cimmaron growled under her breath and hurried away to serve another group of space jockeys before Tamaki beat her to it and received the credit tips instead of her.

Tamaki hadn't had so much fun for ages. A buzz of sexual awareness fizzed through him like the bubbles of a newly opened flask of *vroom*. He pulled a goblet of frothy *veeno*, glancing down the bar at the golden female who filled his mind increasingly with each passing cycle. A subtle golden glow emanated from her skin, giving away her turbulent state of mind. She was just as aware of him as he was of her. In that instant, he made up his mind to follow a new stratagem. Trying to remind himself he was her boss wasn't working. They could have one more date without invoking the mate thing. Just one more taste and then he'd back off and leave her alone.

He could always lend her the passage to leave Marchant. Even if she didn't pay him back and he never saw her again, it would stop the temptation crowding his brain each time he looked at her. Tamaki considered his idea from all angles before nodding. Yeah. That's what he'd do. One more time. If that was what she wanted too...

The rest of the session trickled past so slowly he wanted to roar his frustration aloud. It was pure luck he'd chosen to wear a long tunic instead of his normal form-fitting shirt. At least the tunic covered his bulging groin from curious eyes. His frustration levels, however, remained high.

Finally, security saw the last customers from the club, and they finished the cleanup, ready for the next session.

"Cimmaron, can I have a quick word before you leave?" Tamaki held his breath, wondering how to handle things should she argue about staying.

She cast him a doubtful look, clearly hesitating before finally turning back.

Tamaki waited until the last employee left.

"I wondered if you'd like to see upstairs." He waited, wanting to grin at the expressions dancing across her face. Eagerness. Suspicion. Doubt.

"There's no one up there."

"That's where you're wrong. The rooms are still in use."

Cimmaron straightened abruptly, her golden brows almost meeting when she scowled. "You lie."

Tamaki offered his hand. "Come and see."

Instead of accepting his touch, she brushed past him and stomped up the spiral staircase. The thud of her boots echoed in the empty club.

A victory of sorts. Shaking his head, he followed. Maybe he should've cajoled her into a wager. He took a moment to admire the curvy butt that swayed beneath the short blue uniform skirt. His lips pursed in a silent whistle. Oh yeah, baby.

CHAPTER SIX

He lied, but she had no idea why. Cimmaron headed for the nearest room. Unlike last time, the privacy screen was open. A sapphire glow emanated through the window, lighting up the passage with the shimmering light and shading everything with a delicate blue. Cimmaron stepped closer, near enough to peer into the room and see the occupants. She gasped. The Usplop she'd served downstairs was floating in the air, his limbs secured by stout bindings so he couldn't move. The glow came from his body, and his tentacles undulated, sticking out from his body at right angles. A female—well, Cimmaron thought it was a female—licked delicately at the tentacles sticking out from his groin. An audible moan of pleasure sounded through speakers on either side of the window.

Tamaki stood beside her, not touching but close enough for her to feel the warmth coming off his body. "Our friend has found a suitable partner."

"Yes," Cimmaron answered in a faint voice. Heat suffused her body, yet she couldn't tear her gaze off the intimate scene in front of her.

"Do you like to watch?"

"No!"

"Some people do. I like to watch sometimes, but mainly, I'm an action man."

"The male doing the fucking?" Cimmaron asked tartly, her gaze finally snapping off the couple to glare at him.

"I wouldn't have put it quite like that, but yeah. I'd rather run my hands across your body than watch another couple making love."

"What is this place?" Cimmaron's gaze slid from his face, unable to maintain eye contact without giving away the desire simmering inside her. She refused to succumb to his...his...charm again.

"It's a mating club. Beings from all over the universe and beyond come to meet others. Some date while others like the Usplop are looking for a mate." Tamaki placed his hands on her shoulders and turned her so he could see her face clearly. "If a couple meets in the rooms once or twice, it's considered a date. Should the couple meet a third time, they become mates."

Cimmaron gasped, searching his face desperately for truth, her gut hollowing with fear. "We...we've dated?" She was a Dlog, preprogrammed to mate. If that wasn't bad enough, she'd managed to land in the one place that could make her life miserable—a dating and mating club.

"Yes." Tamaki took her arm. "Would you like to see the other rooms?"

No. Not really. It was difficult enough resisting Tamaki without being tempted by spending time with him. Cimmaron attempted to shake her head, but his sexy grin distracted her. Her mind took a sharp turn into Temptation City. Her pulse pounded a little faster, a fraction louder, and her sex moistened. Tamaki took her arm and drew her deeper into temptation and trouble. She shuddered, trying not to breathe in his enticing scent.

"There are twelve rooms in total. We started with five and have gradually added to the number to increase the club's capacity."

"I don't need to see any more." She dug in her heels, so he stopped his casual saunter down a wide passage.

"But you were curious."

Sure, and now Cimmaron knew what had befallen the curious cat.

Trouble.

Tamaki kept walking, and her steps dragged as she unwillingly followed.

"Okay, I get it. This is punishment."

"No, that is punishment," he said, pointing to another glass window.

There was no glow from this window, and the room inside was very different. Sumptuous and hung with rich red velveteen fabric, there was a huge bed with a gold and crimson cover and lots of plump cushions. Two clubbers inhabited the room. As Cimmaron watched, the female swished a flogger through the air. It struck the male's back, and he fell forward on the bed. She could see his face, but instead of the pain she expected, his face was screwed up in an expression of ecstasy. Her gaze flicked down his body in the *microts* it took him to sprawl facedown on the bed. His cock was fully erect. Cimmaron glanced at Tamaki and found he watched her closely.

"Seen enough?"

Heck, she'd seen enough after the first couple. She gulped. The shrinkton fabric of her uniform was faulty. The material had drawn so tight she could scarcely breathe. Cimmaron nodded because she didn't trust herself to speak without begging him to run his hands across her breasts.

"I need to check the new room. The final electrical work was done tonight, and I want to see if they left it clean and tidy." Without waiting for an answer, Tamaki took her arm again and propelled her in the direction of the new room. Her breath hitched, and she wished he'd quit with the touching. It made her nerve endings sing and jump about as if they were at a dance party. Very unsettling indeed.

After directing her down the passage, Tamaki opened the door to the room and tugged her inside. Dropping her arm, he turned in a slow circle.

"What do you think of the room?"

Cimmaron gave the green color scheme a cursory glance, keeping her attention well away from the bed in the center of the floor. "It's very nice." An understatement. The room reeked of class and status with its beautiful and innovative furnishings.

The desire to shove Tamaki onto the bed struck her without warning. She had to curl her hands into fists to stop from reaching for his broad shoulders. Her Dlog genes. *Again.*

"I'm pleased with the end result. You didn't see all the technological advances the last time you were here." He wrapped his arm around her waist, squeezing her lightly.

"Stop touching me," Cimmaron said and jumped away from him. Her pulse rate surged into an alarming gallop. "I... Just don't touch me."

"Why? What are you frightened of? I'd never hurt you."

The male might look innocent, but she didn't believe it for a moment. "You might not hurt me, but you're ready to have sex," Cimmaron said with a bite in her tone. "I don't want a mate. I'm a pilot. It's what I do."

"I don't know why you're so bent out of shape." His brows rose in a teasing manner. "I was going to show you the room's features. I don't recall mentioning sex." Tamaki tugged on a handle. A drawer slid silently from the wall—a different one than last time.

Despite herself, Cimmaron craned her neck for a better view. An array of sex toys—at least, she presumed they were sex toys since some of them were mystery items with knobs and buttons and jutting swells.

She kept her gaze averted from Tamaki since the desire to run her hands over his body was a torturous litany in her mind. Even so, curiosity had her closing the distance between them to study the sex toys, and before she was aware of issuing the mental command, she touched his face. Her gaze darted to his, and she swallowed at the blaze of return passion in his eyes.

Tamaki jerked her into his arms and plundered her mouth. When she gasped, he took advantage and slid his tongue between her parted lips. He tasted hot and very masculine. With a groan, she stroked his tongue with hers, reveling in his heady taste, the play of teeth, and the dark sound he made deep in his throat. His scent mesmerized her. It was as seductive as his taste—rich, green, redolent of the outdoors.

Their clothes melted away, and they fell onto the large bed. With increasingly urgent hunger they tasted each other, limbs tangling, desire exploding between them.

Cimmaron guided his cock to her and he pushed inside one tiny increment at a time until he impaled her fully. They rocked together, the sensation building rapidly until the pleasure overwhelmed her, and she exploded with the force of her release. The ripples in her pussy continued for long moments, clasping tight to his cock. He groaned, thrust several times in deep, fast strokes before freezing fully embedded in her pussy.

Cimmaron felt the spurt of his seed, gloried in his moan of release. She clutched him, squashed by his weight but enjoying the intimacy of being in his arms.

Tamaki slipped from her moist sex and turned on the bed, pulling her into his arms. He kissed her, a slow and lingering mating of lips. Her hands dropped to cup his buttocks, her fingers delving between his cheeks to massage his puckered rosette.

"Again?" he asked in a husky voice.

Cimmaron nipped at the delicate skin of his neck and waggled an impudent finger, pressing into his anus. She felt his erection spring to life with renewed vigor and smiled against his neck as she moved her hips against him. The hunger remained and only he could appease it.

"Yes, again," she whispered. "I ache. You will fix this. But first, I want to explore you." She pushed him flat on the bed and started to investigate his body. Her hands mapped his muscular chest, her mouth kissed his flat nipples, traced the whorls of his tattoo, and she took the time to tease him before moving lower. He tasted of freshness and smelled of cleansing suds. An addictive combination.

When she grasped his shaft and licked along his swollen cock, he threaded his fingers through her hair. The faint tug brought pain but anchored her too. Her nostrils flared, taking in his mouthwatering scent again. Slowly, she guided him to her mouth and savored her first taste of him.

"Cimmaron." The tone of his voice told her how much he liked and enjoyed the intimacy. It encouraged her to take him deeper, to lick the thick crown of his cock. His trust made her feel powerful and yet feminine too. She sucked hard, drawing him deep and coaxing drops of pre-come from his tip.

"Your mouth feels good, but I want to come inside your pussy this time."

Cimmaron pulled back, releasing him with a popping sound. She'd never wanted to please a man as she wanted to please Tamaki. She smiled and crawled up his body to mash their mouths together in a desperate kiss. Gripping her hips, he lifted her, and she helped him guide his cock to her entrance. A sigh whispered from her as he filled her in exactly the way she craved.

His hands danced across her body, creating magic with each caress. She groaned softly, silently encouraging him to dance a seductive tango with her. All she could think about was touching Tamaki and making love with him all night long.

"I had to call for backup," the security guard said the next evening. "I've never seen the like. Not even in *vroom* addicts, and you know how violent they can get."

Tamaki listened to him, frowning through his explanations of the brawl in the new room on the second floor. The security guard was his best one, but this morn he bore battle scars. Red streaked his bulbous eyes, and an angry scratch marred the scales on one of his cheeks. His tunic was in complete disarray, which was highly unusual in the warrior species renowned for their fastidious natures.

Tamaki tapped a quill against a piece of reusable transmit parchment and ignored the splotches of black that splattered across the pristine white. "I understand the couple who hired the room had a violent disagreement and came to blows."

The security guard nodded then winced. "Yeah. It was a Clart and a Martian, both relatively peaceful races. The Clart female battered the Martian until he lost consciousness. She left via the travel tubes before my team had a chance to intervene."

"Probably the influence of the full moons."

His security guard nodded, and Tamaki hoped he was right. They needed the green room for financial viability. He'd had to fight to grab his slice of trade from the other entertainment businesses on Marchant, and he wasn't about to take backward steps when the club was doing so well.

"Rico and I will double-check the equipment in case it's a malfunction causing the problem." The threesome between Rico, Cimmaron and him hadn't exactly been normal. Hell, Rico still refused to look him directly in the eye whenever they were in the same room.

An abrupt tap sounded on his door before it opened. Rico peered in and relaxed when he saw the security guard.

"Everything seems fine out in the bar. I thought I'd take a ten-min break," Rico said.

Tamaki nodded. "What about upstairs? Is the new room in use?"

Rico tensed and wouldn't meet his gaze. "Yeah. No problems."

The communicator on the security guard's belt beeped without warning, breaking the uncomfortable silence. The male glanced down and silenced the piercing sound. "Problem, boss. Second floor."

They glanced at each other before erupting into action. Tamaki and Rico raced after the security guard, taking the stairs up the spiral staircase two at a time. They turned left to head for the new room. It was empty when they arrived. Two ashen-faced security guards waited, silent sentries either side of the door to the green room.

"What happened?" Tamaki demanded.

"Two females hired the room. They left before we could grab them," one said.

The other shuddered. "There was oozing green blood everywhere. They had sex but it was brutal."

Something worse than full moons was afoot here. Cursing under his breath, Tamaki issued orders. "Tell the females on reception we're not hiring out this room again tonight. Rico, schedule the cleaning droid to do the new room first." He waited for the security guard to leave before returning to his office. Rico followed, and once they were both inside, Tamaki shut the door.

He waved a hand at Rico. "Take a seat." He started speaking again before Rico had taken possession of a chair. Thankfully, his matter-of-fact behavior put his friend at ease. "What do you think the problem is? Any ideas?"

"Most clubbers who enter the room seem to want to have sex." Rico looked him straight in the eye for the first time since the torrid threesome in the new room. "Even though it's not what they would've done normally."

Tamaki sighed, his rapid tapping with the quill sending another shower of black over the once-clean parchment. "It seems that way." He thought of his second bout of sex with Cimmaron and coughed to clear his throat. The sensation jolted the length of his body, making him all too aware of the way he reacted to the Dlog female.

Two dates. One more time, and they'd be mates.

Tamaki wasn't sure how he felt about that. A club manager moved around often, which was why most of them only dated when they took advantage of the club's amenities. And never with staff because of the rules. He'd botched up both the dating thing and the rules. *Good going, hotshot.*

"Tamaki!"

Tamaki jerked to attention. "What?"

"Are you all right?" Rico appeared ready to bolt.

Tamaki chuckled. "Relax. I'm not about to jump you."

"Yeah, my head knows that, but I can't help it. I've never done anything like we did the other night." He glanced at Tamaki and grinned suddenly. "Not before I met Marianna either."

"Yeah. Me neither. Come on. We'd better check out the room."

"Uh-uh. Not in my job description," Rico said. "I don't get paid danger money."

"We'll wear masks and full suits. It has to be something in the atmosphere that's making everyone act that way."

The room appeared warm and welcoming, which was exactly what they'd intended when they drew up the plans and decided on fitting it out.

Tamaki smirked at his friend through the transparent mask he wore over his face. He pushed open the door and stepped inside, his suit rustling loudly. The room looked normal. Tamaki turned to speak to Rico. His friend stood just outside the door, his pale and sweaty face evident even through the mask.

"Coward," Tamaki taunted.

Rico nodded and flapped his arms like a chicken. "*Bawk, bawk, bawk, bawk.*"

"I don't feel anything weird." Tamaki strode over to the controls and examined them. His fingers flew over the keyboard as he typed in commands. "Nothing wrong that I can see. You're the expert with the electronics. Come and take a look."

Rico brushed past him and ran the electronics through a series of self-tests. "Everything looks fine."

"Do you feel anything?" Tamaki ventured.

"Nothing. Do you think it's the suits? That would mean the problem really is transmitted through the life-force conditioners."

Rico studied the unit that pumped suitable breathing life force for each species through the room before glancing at Tamaki. The expression on Tamaki's face brought a scowl. "Aw, shit. I can read your mind. We're going to test it."

"There's already gossip about the room. It's best if we keep as much in-house as possible before we lose customers. We'll prop the door open. If you feel anything weird, get out."

"Fuck," Rico said, but he propped the door open and strode to the middle of the room. "You go first."

Tamaki took a deep breath. His gut crawled with apprehension despite his casual attitude. He wasn't too happy about the situation himself. He counted silently to three and ripped off his mask. Seconds later, Rico did the same. They stared at each other in total silence. Tamaki took another cautious breath. The life force they were breathing seemed okay. There were no weird scents.

Without warning, it hit. A wave of lust that buckled his knees with its intensity. "Out," he gasped.

"But I want..." Rico backed up, his eyes glowing with desperate need. "Don't wanna seem overfamiliar," he ground out, his face screwed up in torment. "But you have the sexiest butt."

"Marianna," Tamaki gasped. He jerked his gaze off Rico and struggled with the multitude of feelings crashing through his body. His blood thundered through his veins. His heart slammed against his ribs, and his hands shook with the need to stroke Rico's face, his skin. He wanted to kiss his friend in the worst way.

Wasn't gonna happen. Was. Not. Going. To. Happen. "Out," he ordered. "You first."

Rico edged toward the door, but Tamaki could see it was a huge struggle. Rico swallowed loudly and licked his lips. Tamaki followed the movement avidly before he realized what he was doing. He ripped his gaze away, his body in a hot sweat. His cock thrust against the coveralls he wore, reminding him of the urgency to mate. The thought pierced his confused brain. If he weren't damn careful, he'd end up mated to his best friend. "Out!" he hollered.

The blast of sound prodded Rico to action. He attempted to walk but fell. With an anguished groan, he crawled across the synwood floor. Tamaki watched his slow progress and fought the urge to race across to his friend and drag him into his arms.

Aghast at the direction of his thoughts, he attempted to dredge up Cimmaron's face. Her almond-shaped eyes and the flash of gold that captivated him every time he saw her. He fought his need to go to Rico, concentrating on Cimmaron and how she felt in his arms, the smooth flow of skin across skin, the glide of lips. Her taste. Tamaki shuddered. Oh yeah. She tasted mighty fine.

Suddenly, the blinding need for sex died. He inhaled deeply and turned to the door. Rico stood just outside the room, gulping in huge drafts of fresh life force.

"You okay?" Tamaki called.

"I am now. You?"

"As soon as you were outside, the urge to mate stopped."

Rico scowled. "Houston, we have a problem."

Rico plonked onto a chair in front of Tamaki's desk and stretched his legs out in front of him. "Business is down on the second level."

"Yeah. The receptionist said it had been quiet. The rumors are flying faster than a Naxmus fighter ship." Tamaki leaped to his feet and paced back and forth behind his desk. "If only I could find the cause. It's ticking me off. I know the problem is something to do with the life-force conditioning unit, but I've changed the machine, the filters, and every other conceivable part. If I'm on my own, I'm fine, but the moment someone else enters the room, all I can think of is sex." Tamaki paused. "You don't want to know what I nearly did to the droid," he added wryly.

"What are you going to do?" Rico asked.

Tamaki sat on the corner of the desk and was pleased his friend didn't jump out of his skin. Things were almost back to normal now that they knew their behavior had been chemically induced somehow. "I'll be upstairs in the room. I've been leaving the door open while there are no customers around, so if you need me, holler from the door. I thought I'd go through everything once more before I go to the experts. You don't need me down here."

"No, we're fine. I didn't approve of hiring Cimmaron initially, but she's a damn fine bartender. Patronage has increased on this level since she arrived."

A pang of jealousy shot through Tamaki. While Rico had finally returned to normal behavior, Cimmaron was avoiding him. Normally he would have taken it on the chin, mentally shrugged, and moved on. After all, what did he want with a mate? He didn't need problems with his bosses or termination of his contract for fraternization. Yet a part of his mind hungered for her touch, her laugh and smile.

God, he missed her sassy tongue and no-nonsense plain speaking. Cimmaron didn't play games, which was why he was trying to do the right thing and keep away. It wasn't easy when she continually dwelled in his mind.

CHAPTER SEVEN

C immaron let herself out the front door of the boarding house and pulled the door shut, tugging to test it was firmly closed. The local youths were in their normal place on the steps of an old warehouse. They had taken to calling her names whenever she passed, but the harassment didn't go further than the insults. She marched past, her nose proudly tilted upward, but not far enough she wasn't aware of her surroundings. The leader sneered, and Cimmaron allowed her upper lip to curl with answering disdain. Childish but necessary if she wanted to win the silent battle waging between them.

"Hear there trouble at club," he called.

His friends cackled like a group of broody Martian hens, nudging each other with their elbows. The leader smirked proudly, puffing up like a Martian rooster keeping his hens in line.

"Don't know what you're talking about," Cimmaron said, barely breaking stride.

"I hear sex good in new room."

His smug satisfaction, his knowing tone, made her halt and turn to scan his face.

"Good trickie, *chica*, huh? Don't get mad, get even."

Without thought, Cimmaron prowled toward him, ready to choke the truth from his scrawny neck. If he knew anything, she'd get it from him. Damn, she'd had sex twice with Tamaki in that room. *Twice.*

Not sex, a small voice hummed at the back of her mind. *Made love.*

She cursed under her breath, her eyes narrowing as a wave of rage swept her. She didn't want a mate. She would *not* mate, no matter how sexy or how enticing Tamaki was or how he made her motor purr. Her job was pilot, and she intended to fly ships.

The youth's friends backed away in alarm, leaving the leader isolated—alone and the target of her wrath.

Cimmaron advanced again, stopping close enough for her to smell the *vroom* fumes exiting with each uneasy breath the leader took. She inhaled and gagged at the stench of sweaty bodies. They obviously subscribed to the latest fad idea—the school of thought regarding cleanliness as unhealthy. She breathed through her mouth, closing out the worst of the reek of unwashed bodies, *vroom* fumes, and fear.

"Tell me," she gritted out, impatient for answers. She glanced at her timepiece and scowled. Time was wasting. "Tell me now."

"Bitch," the leader growled, and before she could grab him, he whirled away. He melted into the shadowed alley that ran between the buildings, followed closely by his friends.

"*Phrull.*" Cimmaron stared after them for a moment before deciding she'd better head for the club. She'd worm the truth out of them the next time she saw them.

Cimmaron stalked past locals laden with produce who were leaving the late-night market. Did the youths know something or had they heard rumors and decided to capitalize on them? She replayed his words as she dodged a pair of droids pulling a cart laden with Marchant dried vegetables and dehydrated fruits. The leader had talked about revenge. He looked the type who didn't forgive easily, especially with his pride involved. She gave her timepiece another glance and broke into a run. On arrival at the club, she scanned her finger, and the door opened to let her inside.

"Late," Hulk said.

Cimmaron sneered at him, and Hulk glowered right back. She bit back the urge to grin. The male carried photos of his offspring in his currency belt. She'd caught him showing them to the other security guards. She shook her head, bemusement making her frown. The offspring looked ugly, and she didn't get why he was so proud, even though his behavior was kinda cute.

"You coming in, or ya gonna stay there?"

"I work here," Cimmaron snapped, instantly more comfortable with their usual repartee. "'Course I'm coming in." She strode past Hulk and headed for the changing rooms where she'd left her thigh-high boots. In the dressing room, she slipped out of her coat, pulled off her pilot boots and thrust her feet into the hated uniform boots.

She sighed before heading back out to the bar. Her currency didn't seem to grow much. The pills to suppress her Dlog hormones had arrived at the apothecary a few pars earlier. They were expensive, but she had to have them. Without the pills all her plans would turn to solar dust. At this rate, she was going to remain stranded for many more moon cycles. "Bloody male."

"Talking about me?"

Cimmaron came to an abrupt halt but not quite quick enough. Her breasts brushed the hard wall of Tamaki's chest before she jerked away. Frissons of heat ricocheted through her body, traveling through her breasts and lower to her sex. She gasped, trying to control her wayward hormones. A soft chuckle snapped up her head, and she glared at him.

"Don't touch me."

"I didn't mean to. I thought you saw me coming."

She bit the inside of her lip in consternation. She should have noticed him standing there. Working in this bar was making her pilot instincts fade, turning her soft and girlie.

"I'm late," she snapped.

Tamaki merely grinned. "I don't think the boss will dock your currency earnings. Do you want to have dinner with me?"

Cimmaron gaped at the very idea. "No."

Tamaki reached out and brushed his hand over her cheek before she had an inkling of what he intended. Another series of lightning bolts shot through her body until she finally reacted and stepped away. It was becoming difficult to resist him. So hard, when he smiled at her, his eyes crinkling at the corners. Her thoughts constantly drifted to him, and she...she liked him, enjoyed spending time with him, verbally sparring and the kisses...

"You have to eat. Besides, I don't want to mate with you," Tamaki said. "I thought we were friends, and you might like to share a meal."

"I don't have friends." What was wrong with the man? Why wouldn't he leave her alone? Every other male she encountered backed off once she'd made it clear she wasn't interested. Also glowering helped, except her scowls didn't work on Tamaki. He just grinned, melting her militant mood and molding it into pleasure and acceptance instead.

"I'm your friend, Cimmaron. I'm going to work in the green room. Page me when you're on a dinner break, and I'll come down." Raising a hand in farewell, he walked away, leaving her staring after him.

The loud buzz of a Marchant midge made her realize her mouth hung open in invitation. She snapped it shut so the insect didn't fly inside and hurried off to the bar, trying to outrun her jumbled thoughts.

"You're late," Rico said.

"Blame Tamaki. He wanted to talk." *Phrull*, he wanted to be friends. Cimmaron shook away her horror. "What do ya want?" she said to a waiting pilot.

His teasing gaze slid across her bared skin and the tight uniform before settling on her scowling face. He sighed. "I guess I'm gonna have to settle for a drink. An Earth whiskey. No ice."

Cimmaron nodded and turned to fix the pilot's drink. After sliding the drink across the bar, she accepted the handful of credits he gave her. She moved on to the next customer, her mind still on the male she'd just served. He was much prettier than Tamaki, and he had music in his drawl. He hadn't caused a single blip on her hormone radar while Tamaki— She broke off the thought to slam a flask of *vroom* on the bar, splashing a few drops over the shiny surface. It sizzled on contact before turning a milky white color, then pink when the flash of lights caught it. "Sorry," she said to the customer as she ran a cloth over the spill.

She moved to the next customer, ignored the attempts at flirting while she hummed along with the live band. Not bad for a change. The laughter became louder, more raucous as the night passed. She took her break and didn't page Tamaki as he'd requested. Guilt assailed her briefly, but she shoved it away, telling herself she didn't have time for a long break. They needed her back behind the bar because it was so busy. Time passed and, eventually, the punters started to leave in twos or threes, wobbling unsteadily through the door into the frigid Marchant morn.

Cimmaron swiped an errant lock of hair from her face and wearily started to restock the drinks behind the bar. On the other side, droids collected empty flasks and goblets, stacking them on the bar for washing.

"Have you seen Tamaki?" Rico asked.

"No." She pushed aside the tiny bit of hurt that flashed through her. He hadn't meant the friend thing. Friendship wasn't possible, not since she was a Dlog. Dlog females didn't have friends. They had mates.

"He's not answering his page, and we need him to sign off on the stock and send the transmission to head office."

"Send security to get him." Cimmaron scanned the remaining customers who were finishing off drinks. A curse echoed through the club. "*Phrull*, those idiots are gonna fight."

Rico ran a hand through his hair, making it stand up in tufts. "I'd better help security. Go and get Tamaki. Remind him he needs to do the sign off."

"Yeah. Okay."

Rico grabbed her forearm as she passed. "Don't go inside the room. Speak to Tamaki from the door."

"Why can't someone else go?" Cimmaron frantically searched for a way out. Avoidance was best. Every time she came within touching distance of the sexy male, she wanted more. She wanted taste as well as sight. She wanted...

Phrull!

"Go, Cimmaron," Rico ordered, and before she could rally another argument, he leaped across the bar and waded into the skirmish.

A chair crashed over on its side. Hulk grabbed two beings by the scruffs of their necks and threw them toward the door.

Cimmaron dodged a groaning Vercops. His eyes bulged from their sockets—all six of them—while shrill distress calls from his mate filled the air. She ran up the stairs, her boots clunking noisily with each step. At the top of the spiral staircase, she turned to the left and hurried to the green room.

The *microt* she spied the privacy screen for the green room, her heart started to pump faster. Something close to alarm prickled the hairs at the back of her neck. She halted outside the dense metal door. It was shut too. She reached for the door handle and hesitated. She wiped her moist palm on her shrinkton skirt and tried again.

"*Phrull*," she whispered when her hand trembled violently. Each time she saw Tamaki, it was harder to resist his good-natured charm. And the longing... The longing grew stronger and stronger. She was a pilot, dammit. She threw her shoulders back and thrust open the door.

"Tamaki." Cimmaron cleared her throat and repeated his name in a firmer voice. "Tamaki. Are you there?"

The fight downstairs was escalating. A loud crash echoed up the stairs. A male roared in his native tongue, the shrieks and clicks sounding fierce and furious.

Cimmaron peered around the corner. Someone was sprawled

on the floor. All she could see was legs, but she thought it was Tamaki. "Tamaki?" No answer. Her brows drew together in a frown. She was going to have to go inside. Gingerly, she entered the room, holding her breath.

Tamaki was out cold, and for some reason, he'd ripped off all his clothes. She skimmed her hands over his naked body but could see nothing to indicate a wound. "Tamaki." She shook him, and he groaned.

The scuff of feet overhead made her jerk her head upward. A ceiling tile wasn't on straight. She caught a flash of color. Someone was up there.

"Come down here, coward."

A laugh resounded. Cimmaron froze. She knew that laugh.

"Not so smarti nowa, *chica*," a voice sneered.

"Cimmaron, you shouldn't be here," Tamaki said in a groggy voice. He pushed to a sitting position. "Man, my head hurts. I heard a noise, but before I could turn around, someone zapped me with a stun gun. So hot in here."

"You have no wounds," Cimmaron said, staring into his beautiful blue eyes.

"I have a headache."

They stared at each other for a long moment, and suddenly her uniform felt heavy and burdensome.

"God, you're beautiful."

"All Dlog are beautiful," she countered. To cover her sudden confusion, she traced the whorls of his tattoo with her finger. *Phrull*, was that flirtatious tone her? She shook her head in an attempt to clear it, but all she could think of was Tamaki and how his cock felt buried deep inside her body.

Tamaki smiled and placed his hand on her thigh, running his

fingers over the naked skin between her thigh-high boots and her skirt. His hand was warm and sent a shower of tingles surfing through her body.

Their gazes met, and it seemed as if a gossamer cord drew them closer. She swallowed, the sound loud inside the quiet room. Tamaki's fingers continued to stroke her thigh until a purr erupted from deep in her throat. They shouldn't do this. She should leave. His fingers stroked across and up, edging to the plain regulation panties she wore. Her skin color deepened to a brilliant gold.

"We need to leave the room. Now. Before something happens." Cimmaron thought about standing and leaving. She tensed for a scant *microt,* intending to move, then Tamaki's finger slipped beneath the leg binding of her panties. It moved with unerring accuracy, stroking moist flesh and grazing across her clitoris. She sucked in a hasty breath, the ribbons of sensation making her body arch with pleasure.

"Do you want more?" Tamaki whispered, his breath warm against her ear. "I do."

A sneering laugh rang out, jolting them both from the sensual web binding them together. They jumped to their feet and stared up at the ceiling. A fine mist showered down on their heads before the scurry of feet made it clear their watcher had retreated.

Cimmaron gulped, trying to retain the return to sanity, but Tamaki touched her. He trailed his hand across her bare belly. She shivered, losing the fight for reason and leaned into him so her breasts brushed his chest. Her nipples tightened to hard, achy points, and she stroked her hand down his cheek and chin.

"I want more." A tiny voice at the back of her mind protested for an instant until Tamaki leaned in and kissed her, stealing her breath as he traced the curve of her lips with his tongue. She gasped at the jolt of sensation, and he took advantage, deepening their kiss. Slowly, he explored her mouth until pleasure coursed through her body. He tasted of spearmint tonight, of spicy heat and male. His muscles flexed beneath her questing hands, and the bulge at his groin pressed into her lower body.

Tamaki pulled away to glance down at her with a grin. "I believe I can give you more." He tugged at the cloth covering her breasts, expertly removing it before she had time to blink. He let the blue strip drop to the floor and traced the delicate veins visible beneath the surface of her skin. "You're so beautiful."

His fingers drifted across her collarbone and dropped to cup her breasts. He pinched one nipple until it turned a deeper gold. A sharp tug brought a corresponding pain. A good ache that made her cry out for more and arch her body into his touch. Between her legs, her moist folds grew wetter, her body needier. Her heart lurched painfully as the hard ridge of his cock pressed into her belly.

Without warning, he scooped her off her feet and carried her to the large bed. She bounced lightly before Tamaki covered her, his bulk preventing her from moving again.

"Kiss me, Tamaki. Touch me. Please."

"Oh, I intend to," he promised, and trailed his hands and mouth across her hipbone.

Cimmaron sucked in her breath at the tingle of teeth and the drag of roughened fingertips when he explored her body. She smelled his hot male scent and reveled in his touch. She parted her legs for him as he silently requested, her folds engorged and wet, so wet. "Tamaki."

She shifted restlessly as he tested her readiness, his thumb teasing the sensitive nub nestled at her core. A jolt of pleasurable excitement made her breath catch.

Tamaki laughed softly. His invasive fingers drove her higher as they pumped deep inside her. They brushed and teased her clit. Fire whipped her sensitized body. He slipped his hands beneath her buttocks, lifting her to his mouth. His tongue teased her swollen flesh, flailing her clit and driving the sensations in her impossibly higher. She sucked in a deep breath, releasing it on a moan. By the goddess, his touch felt good. He delved between her legs, stoking her need higher but not giving her enough pressure for release.

"Tamaki, please." *Phrull*, she never begged, but she wanted to right now.

"You're wet and swollen for me. Your skin glows gold and gleams for my possession." He sounded smug, and she sensed rather than saw his grin. He pressed a kiss to her inner thigh, the stubble on his lean cheeks rasping against her soft skin. His tongue journeyed the length of her cleft, making her shudder with helpless need.

"Yes," she whispered, a purr rumbling deep in her throat.

With one final lap of her clit, Tamaki moved up her body. He kissed her lips, and she could taste her essence on his tongue. Desperate to have her pussy filled, she pushed him onto his back and impaled herself on his cock, increment by increment. She groaned and rode him, driving them both closer to fulfillment. His cock seemed to grow larger with each lazy swivel of her hips until he crammed her impossibly full.

He reached out to capture her breast with his hands before taking her in his mouth, drawing sweet circles around her nipple with his tongue. His eyes were a deep, dark blue, and they caressed each part of her as she swayed above him. He made her feel beautiful. He made her feel powerful. Tamaki made her feel like a woman—a woman worthy of him.

As desire flared between them, her pace quickened. Tamaki rose to meet each downward stroke. Sensation grew, tingles spreading outward until she convulsed, coming with hard pulses of her pussy. Deep in her womb, she felt the spurt of his seed. She heard his groan of completion and fell forward until she rested against his chest, panting to regain her breath. Tamaki's arms came around her, holding her so close she was aware of the thunder of his heart.

Cimmaron soaked up the novelty of being close to a male and the sense of rightness at being with this male. She didn't want to move.

"Oh my God. You two have been at it again." Rico hovered in the doorway, strain darkening his face.

Cimmaron let out a squeak, one that had no business coming from her throat. She scowled at the un-pilot-like sound and attempted to hide her naked body behind Tamaki's greater bulk. He merely chuckled and drew her close so her breasts squished against his chest.

Then he stretched, looking like a lazy cat, supremely at ease with his nakedness. "Yeah. Life is good."

Rico raked his hand through his dark hair. "That's three times."

"Four actually." No mistaking the smug tone in his voice.

The sensual fog was starting to clear from her mind. Cimmaron stiffened, and her eyes narrowed.

"Thrice a mate," Rico said.

Cimmaron let out a screech that made Rico wince. Mated? They were *phrullin'* mated? She thumped Tamaki over the shoulder, but the lazy lug merely grinned.

"Great, isn't it?" He pressed a kiss to her bare shoulder and eyed her heaving breasts with interest.

"But I've been taking pills." The words came out as a wail of horror. All her currency spent to keep her free of a male, to help her resist Tamaki. She was mated, mated to the smug male, despite all her careful steps to remain free. She wanted to qualify as a pilot, not act the slave for some bossy male. *Phrull*, the idea of popping out offspring every solar annum made her want to upchuck.

"No!" She yanked from Tamaki's grip. The instant they were no longer touching, she felt a physical wrench in her gut. She took several steps away from the bed, aware of the pull to return to his side intensifying. The desperate need to touch him and reassure herself brought a scowl. They couldn't be mated. They couldn't.

"I'm so sorry, Cimmaron," Rico said, his voice edged with painful sympathy. "There's nothing you can do. You and Tamaki are mated for life."

It was the quiet pain in his voice that made her accept the truth. Cimmaron turned to the male she'd mated with, part of her hating him even as the mating bonds writhed through her blood, tempting her to touch him. For a few seconds, she thought of how much she liked him and spending time with him, the way he pushed her, teased her in a way no other male had ever done before. She shoved the traitorous thoughts aside.

"*Phrull*," she croaked as she took a step toward the bed. "I'm stranded." Her voice held pain, bitterness, frustration, and deep disappointment. "Stranded for life."

Chapter Eight

"No!" Tamaki watched his mate pull on her clothes with quick, efficient movements. He had feelings for her. From the moment they'd met, the yearning to make her his had crept up on him, growing stronger with each passing *microt*. While his mind had told him he shouldn't do this—it was against the rules—his heart had overruled him every time. He'd never wanted another female like this. He... Hell, he loved her. She belonged to him, with him. And somehow, he'd prove it to her. This wasn't just about the mating. He'd felt the longing even before they'd slept together for the third date.

Tamaki watched the flash of bare butt as she hurriedly dressed and her long, luscious legs as she thrust her feet into her boots. He watched the angry swish of her hips when she strode across the room and winced at the strident *tap-tap* of her heels as she departed. Despite it all, he couldn't restrain a grin. His mate was a babe.

"Take that damn smirk off your face," Rico snapped.

Tamaki sat up on the bed and stretched lazily before scratching his belly. His muscles felt well used, but he couldn't wait for another go-round with his mate.

"Did you hear me? You've broken the no-fraternization rule. You'll lose your job, man!"

Tamaki smirked and stood. "I don't think so. Don't dither at the door like a chaperone, Rico. I believe it's safe to enter now."

"No thanks," Rico said with heartfelt sentiment. "I'm not stepping foot in this room until I know for sure it's safe."

"There was someone in the roof. I believe they've been misting a version of Earth's Spanish Fly drug into the air—just enough to make the occupants of the room desperate for sex."

"But Spanish Fly makes you keep going and going like that advertisement on Earth television claims about its batteries. You know—the one with the bunny rabbit." Rico stopped when he saw Tamaki's rising brows. "Or so I've heard."

"I believe this is the version discovered on the planet Talon. You know, the newly discovered planet?"

Rico glanced at his timepiece. "Shit, I came up here to remind you about the reports for head office. They're late. The window for transmission communication is almost closed."

"Hell." Tamaki bound off the bed and hurriedly scrambled into his clothes. "Why didn't you say so?" He sprinted from the room, down the corridor, and literally flew down the spiral staircase. At the base of the stairs, he came to an abrupt halt, and Rico barreled into him from behind. The main bar and seating area was a mess with chairs lying drunkenly on the floor, upturned tables, and broken goblets strewn across the room. A security guard lay flat out on the floor with one of the barmaids squatting beside him. She dabbed at splotches of purple blood on his face and glanced up with a worried expression when they hurried past.

"What happened?"

"There was a fight," Rico said. "Never mind that. We handled it. Get the figures through to HO before the transmission window closes. We don't want an auditor droid landing here. They have no sense of humor."

Tamaki gave a terse nod before striding through to his office. Luckily, the figures were completed and ready to go. He plugged his code into a keypad to hook up with the satellite, and after checking the files were in the send box, he hit the transmit button.

The transfer process started smoothly, and he leaned back in his chair while he considered his problems. Or blessings, he thought with a sudden chuckle. Having Cimmaron as his mate was worth any aggravation he might suffer in his future. He sobered. How the hell was he going to get past the company strictures about fraternization? There were very clear guidelines as Rico had reminded him several times. After the scandal and lawsuit on Mars, all managers and senior staff had to sign the no-fraternization clause. He loved his job and didn't want to give it up, but he had a mate now, for better or worse. They were a team for life.

A done deal.

Tamaki tilted his chair back on two legs, closed his eyes, and concentrated. There must be a way.

His keyboard beeped, and he punched in another code, an added security feature. This shunted the information through the final stage. While the figures were finishing transmitting, Tamaki continued to puzzle about Cimmaron. He liked her very much. He liked being with her and was happy with being mated. *Okay.* He loved her, dammit. A grin broke out. Hell yeah.

He loved her.

The mating process had merely hurried the relationship to a conclusion. Tamaki snorted. Not that Cimmaron would accept defeat. He needed to find a way to make her happy otherwise neither of them would find contentment. But what? How?

An abrupt tap sounded on the door, and Rico walked in. "Did you get the info to head office?"

"Yeah. It's still sending." Tamaki let his chair settle on all four legs. "How are things going with Marianna?"

Rico brightened. "Better. She's accepted my offer to take her to the Marchant picnic on Founder's Day."

Tamaki did an internal eye roll. Man, he hated the pretentious Marchant upper-class sector, and he didn't like Marianna's superior manner either. But since Rico was happy to move in those circles and was steadfastly hooked on Mariana, he wouldn't verbalize his doubts. He studied his friend closely, his mind working at speed. Was it possible?

"I have an idea." Tamaki glanced at the transmitter and tapped his forefinger on the hard surface of the desktop. "Can you stay for a bit longer or are you seeing Marianna?"

"Yeah, I can stay." He didn't add any further explanation, so Tamaki figured Mariana was busy. None of his business, but he thought his friend could do better.

"Okay, listen up," he said. "Here's what I was thinking."

Cimmaron went through the motions of cleaning behind the bar, immersed deep in her thoughts. *Phrullin'* male!

"Where did you disappear to?" Melad asked, breaking into her mental cursing.

She concentrated on a dirty spot on the shiny bar, scrubbing her damp cloth across it with brisk moves. It did nothing to settle her ruffled mood. "Rico asked me to find Tamaki urgently." Her voice was sharp. Defensive. And it gave away almost as much as the color of her skin.

Phrull!

She refrained from looking at Melad, not because she was worried about lying convincingly but because her skin was giving off a golden glow. She knew her eyes would be flashing a brilliant gold, bright enough to dazzle. A sure signal of her emotional state. Anyone with half a brain would guess sex had induced the glow.

"Wish he'd sent me," Melad said in a dreamy voice. With sure, competent moves, she stacked goblets in the sterilizer. "I'd like to know what Tamaki looks like under all those black clothes he wears."

"He's our boss." Thank goodness Melad hadn't seemed to notice anything strange.

Melad's head jerked up. A flash of surprise shot across her face, and Cimmaron forced her lips to a stiff smile to counteract the sharp tone.

"Sorry." Cimmaron sucked in a deep breath, attempting to stuff the surge of jealousy in the far reaches of her mind.

Melad shrugged and turned back to stacking the bronze goblets. She pulled out another rack and stacked the silver goblets separately. Cimmaron resumed her cleaning. Tamaki didn't belong to her despite his assertions they were mates now.

After another inhalation, Cimmaron felt marginally calmer. The answer was simple.

She'd leave.

That's what she'd do. Paying for the suppression pills had cut into her funds, but the tips plus the part of her wages she'd been able to save had added to a decent amount of currency. Maybe she could hire on as a deckhand?

When a Dlog mated, they were planet-bound. This mating was different. It was against her will. She suppressed the blip of excitement as she thought of Tamaki and the way he made her feel when he touched her, when his cock was deeply embedded in her pussy. The way she felt safe and happy whenever she spent time with him as if she belonged for once. She shook herself. No! The mating *was* against her will, dammit.

She couldn't afford to stay here on Marchant, not if she wished to clear her name and graduate to full pilot status. But despite this, Tamaki kept creeping into her mind, and she whirled with a huff of impatience to stock the chillers.

As usual, the *vroom* compartment was totally empty. Cimmaron worked quickly, efficiently stocking the white flasks and other drinks as she made plans. Her mind kept drifting. Tamaki. Tamaki. *Tamaki.*

She picked up an empty crate, stomped from the bar, and slammed it onto the pile awaiting pickup by the local brewer.

A snarl built low in her throat, easing out in a feral growl. That was it. No matter who she had to sign on with or what demeaning job she had to take, she was going to leave Marchant. Despite her craving to find Tamaki, she couldn't settle, not like this, without a fight. She'd battled too hard to overcome her Dlog heritage. She'd depart tonight.

Cimmaron made haste to the boarding house but still took care to keep to the brightly lit streets and alleys the security droids patrolled. At the boarding house, she let herself inside and went directly to her room. After packing the meager belongings she'd accumulated since being on Marchant, she left out enough currency to cover her lodging and scribbled a brief note to Lissa. She dressed in her plain brown tunic, trews, and boots, leaving the blue shrinkton skirt and top on her sleeping mat. The boots were in her locker at the club.

As she let herself out and walked off without looking back, Cimmaron pushed aside the loneliness that suddenly assailed her. Her steps faltered, then she threw her shoulders back and increased her pace. She was used to being alone. Ever since she'd decided to train as a pilot, she'd traveled a solitary road. Once she cleared her name and they reinstated her, the hole wouldn't seem quite as large.

She stalked down the brightly lit streets, but instead of heading for the club, she turned toward the spaceport. Vagrants loitered in the shadowed recesses of buildings. She kept moving in a confident manner, knowing the slightest trace of fear would lead to disaster.

A sudden sharp pang of pain in her chest took her by surprise. She gasped and staggered at its intensity. Clutching her chest, she attempted to breathe through the torture. The shuffle of feet behind her made her spin with an instinctive feral growl. No way was she succumbing to vagrants intent on stealing her possessions and currency.

"Back off," she snarled.

A gnarled and stooped male wrapped in a grubby white cloak held up his hands in a peaceful sign of surrender. "Not me to worry 'bout," he whispered, his voice hoarse from years of smoking the harsh local tobacco. "Rich young males slummin'. Thems cause worry. Hide!" He slipped into the shadows and disappeared from sight.

Cimmaron glanced over her shoulder. *Phrull!* The same group who harassed her most days. Had they followed? She'd been so leery of what was in front of her, she hadn't checked for danger slinking at her rear. She slid into the shadows and hastened her pace, moving swiftly through the dimly lit areas of the rutted streets. A wave of pain crashed through her chest again. *Phrull.* She'd taken a pill before she'd left for work. Determined footsteps behind made her suck up the agony and move.

Dilapidated stalls and areas to display traders' wares were in evidence now. Another bolt of cramp hit, and with a silent grimace, she sank to the ground behind a pile of discarded display tables. Her boot went into an open drain, the splash too loud for her liking. She froze, hoping they hadn't heard.

"Where *chica* go?" a sing-song voice called.

"No see," someone answered. "No see."

"Tricky *chica*. Tricky. Tricky. *Tricky.*" Cimmaron recognized the leader's voice. *Phrull.* Just once, she'd like to level the playing field and confront the coward one-on-one instead of the complete gang. Her top lip curled in contempt. It would never happen—not with his rich parents and their currency behind him.

A spaceship roared overhead, taking off from the spaceport. The flare from the propulsion unit lit the entire street for an instant while the rumble from the engines filled the air. She crouched even lower, glad of her nondescript brown tunic. It would be difficult for them to spot her. All she needed to do was wait them out—if the stench of rotting rat-creatures didn't kill her first.

"*Chica* must 'ave gone other street," the leader said. "Backtrack."

He wasn't going to check behind all the piles of rubble in the street? Surprise made her blink. She'd thought him brighter than that. Or...perhaps he was. She remained where she was for long moments after he'd spoken and she'd heard them retreat. The cold ground cramped her legs, matching the throbbing in her chest. She shifted uneasily, but the pain grew worse. When she was about to move, she heard a soft curse and then footsteps. Cimmaron's heart thundered with sudden apprehension. She'd been right to wait before moving. The leader had tried to smoke her out with trickery.

Pain hit again. She curled up in a tight ball, trying not to make any noise in case they came back. A shiver racked her body. *Phrull.* Cold. So cold. Tamaki would know how to warm her freezing body. As the thought slipped stealthily into her mind, the cramps eased. Cimmaron listened carefully and heard the murmur of voices to her left. The shuffle of feet. The swish of a cloak. She pressed a fist to the nagging ache emanating from her chest and concentrated, trying to discern if it was the gang of youths or others.

"*Psst!*"

Cimmaron threw her head backward and thumped against the stone wall behind her. For a moment, she saw stars. A groan squeezed past her lips as she tried to figure out which part of her hurt worst—her head or her chest.

"*Psst*, they've gone." A male in a dirty white robe appeared in front of her. It was the vagrant she'd seen earlier. "Leave now. Peaceful street. Don't want trouble."

Well, that was telling her. Her presence was not required. "I'm going." Cimmaron turned away from the vagrant and walked quickly to the relative safety of the spaceport.

The agony in her chest intensified, robbing Cimmaron of breath. Clutching her chest, she pushed through the growing throngs of beings exiting and entering the spaceport. The *microt* she entered the port, she made a point of standing straight and pretending her chest didn't hurt like the devil. Once she found paid employment on a ship leaving Marchant, she'd have time to recuperate from whatever ailed her. Meantime, she'd suck it in.

Cimmaron decided she'd go to the workers' canteen first. Gossip was usually the best source when it came to searching for employment. And if she had to use her Dlog looks to gain the information, then so be it. The knot on her head continued to ache in harmony with her chest. A film of sweat broke out on her forehead.

"What happened to you?" a male in oil-stained coveralls said.

Cimmaron frowned. "Nothing." She stuck her nose in the air and attempted to sidle past.

"The side of your head is bleeding."

"Where?" Cimmaron prodded the lump on her head. A sharp pain shot through her head. She winced. Her hand came away bloody. "Oh, that. I hit my head. Tripped," she added. "Are any of the ships hiring?"

"You?"

"No, the king of Viros," Cimmaron snapped. "Of course, it's me."

"Not many beings willing to hire a Dlog. Too much trouble."

Cimmaron drew herself up tall and stared down at him in distaste. "I'm not a Dlog." She maintained his gaze, but it was difficult with the persistent throb in her chest. All she wanted to do was curl up in a ball of misery or, even better, lie down with Tamaki at her side. He would make her forget the pain. They'd touch each other, stroke, fondle. Kiss.

A maintenance droid dropped a tray on the floor with a loud clatter, thankfully yanking Cimmaron from her traitorous thoughts. Tamaki. Bah! The male had set her up. Tricked her. Not that she believed anything about the mate thing. She didn't feel different. A vision of Tamaki formed inside her head, and her whole body jerked, shock freezing her rigid. The bloody male was naked, his erection thrusting outward. He was flaunting himself.

"Are you all right?" the male asked.

Cimmaron shook the vision from her head. "Yes. Anyone hiring?" she demanded out of patience with the male. She'd asked a simple question. Was it too much to expect an answer?

He waved his hand in the direction of the far wall. "Check out the notice board over there."

"Thanks." She walked in the direction he'd indicated. Each step was pure torture. Beads of sweat formed on her brow again even though she'd wiped it earlier, and her meager possessions weighed heavy on her shoulder, as burdensome as two crates of *vroom*. Her chest continued to ache with sharp flashes striking like lashes from a whip. She transferred her scruffy bag to her left hand and raised her right hand to massage her chest.

It didn't help.

With each step she took, the stabbing pangs radiated from her torso. She gasped, her bag dropping from nerveless fingers. It hit the floor, falling in front of a trader. The trader tripped and fell headfirst onto a table laden with trays of Marchant stew and flasks of *vroom* and *reeb*. Crashes and colorful curses filled the air as chairs scraped across the floor, and the beings seated at the table jumped to their feet. A pungent stream of Marchant stew dripped over the edge of the table.

"I'm so sorry." Cimmaron's hand pressed against the middle of her chest but still the pain intensified. She wobbled then crumpled to the ground, her legs unable to support her any longer.

The nearest being, a pilot from one of the freighters judging by his uniform and boots, knelt beside her. "You okay?"

"Looking for job," Cimmaron gasped out, her mind focused on the one thing most important to her. A job. Freedom. Independence.

He touched his palm to her forehead. "You're sick."

"Not. Need job."

"We have a job available. For a pilot. Not a...ah..." The male trailed off while several of the others laughed.

"Not a Dlog concubine," a female pilot said with a disdainful curl of her lip.

"I am a pilot." With great effort, she stood. When she wobbled precariously, the male who'd helped her grabbed and held her upright. "Second pilot on the *Intrepid*."

"Yeah, right," the female countered before turning her back on Cimmaron in a pointed snub. The rest of the pilots did the same.

The male pilot pulled a cloth from his tunic and wiped her forehead. "You're not well. Why don't you find lodgings until you're feeling better? *Phrull*, I hope whatever you have isn't contagious."

"There's nothing wrong with me!" Staying would mean facing Tamaki again. She scowled even though the chest pains had eased a fraction. The stupid male thought they were mates. Yeah. Okay. They'd had a little fun together, but they weren't mates. She'd know if they were since she'd have trouble leaving his side. She'd turn all obedient. Subservient. She'd want to touch him all the time and be touched in return. She'd...

Phrull, she definitely had the touch thing down. Her fingers practically itched with the need to fondle, to run her hand and tongue and lips across his naked torso, across his family tattoo. And lower.

"No one will hire you if you can barely stand."

Cimmaron sighed, aware the male was taking most of her weight. If he let go she'd likely fall flat on her face. "But I need to leave Marchant."

"Not gonna happen." The male checked his timepiece. "Time for me to head back to my ship."

"Thanks." She retrieved her bag and found an empty chair to sink onto before watching the pilot stride away. Envy sat uneasily in her gut. That male was going to fly a ship out of Marchant airspace while, once again, she would remain stranded.

CHAPTER NINE

Tamaki strode down the narrow alley, his lips pursed in a silent whistle. The Marchant morn was cool, and a puff of steam erupted with his exhalation. He drew his cloak around his body to keep the worst of the chill at bay and increased his pace.

Cimmaron. His mate.

He couldn't wait to see her again. First, he'd kiss her golden lips, then he'd swing her into his arms and carry her off to her room where they could be private, their loving as noisy as they wanted. He'd strip her lean yet curvy body of every scrap of clothing. Next, he'd tie her hands and legs with the silken scarves he carried in his pockets so she couldn't move. He'd tease her breasts and nipples until they stood erect, with lots of kissing and nuzzling in between. He'd kiss the vulnerable skin of her neck and behind her ears. He'd draw her taut golden nipples deep into his mouth and suckle.

Gradually, he'd work down her body. Yeah. Tamaki grinned. He'd delve into the dip of her bellybutton with his tongue. She'd be hot for him by this time.

Impatient.

She'd wriggle and twist against the silken scarves that kept her bound. Hell, she might even start to beg. Tamaki chuckled at the thought. Somehow, he didn't think his mate liked begging. She might demand in that imperious way of hers. Captain mode. Life between them would never be smooth-running, but the odd disagreement wouldn't trouble him. They'd function well as a team.

What would he do to her next?

Ah yes. Maybe he'd skip a few parts and stoke her impatience even higher. He'd massage her feet and calves with a delicate-scented cream. Maybe a cream scented with moonflowers and a hint of *jabo* aphrodisiac to make them both even hotter for each other. Desperate.

Tamaki paused to open his cloak to the morn chill because suddenly, he burned with heat. A sharp pain tore through his chest, and Tamaki drew in a harsh breath. Damn, he'd had a cramp in his gut all morn. He breathed through the twinge of pain before continuing his brisk pace. He thumped on the door of Lissa's boardinghouse, his feel-good mood returning once the nagging throb in his chest faded.

The door opened. Tamaki grabbed Lissa in a firm hug and squeezed her until the air hissed from her lungs, and she started to protest.

"Let a lady breathe," she gasped out.

"But it's such a fine morn. Has Cimmaron risen from her slumber?"

"Cimmaron's gone. You'd better come inside." She led him through to her meeting room and gestured him to take a seat. "She left a note."

"Gone where? I didn't think she had enough currency yet." Tamaki sat but jumped to his feet *microts* later and strode from one end of the sumptuous room to the other. He dodged a green velveteen cozy chair and paused briefly to stare through the privacy slats at the windows. His gut churned. He'd thought...

A heartfelt groan emerged. God, with Cimmaron, he should never think or assume. She was so strong and independent. "Gone where?"

"She didn't say. I thought she would have told you since you work together."

"We're mates," Tamaki said bluntly. "I didn't plan for it. The mating happened by mistake, but I can't be sorry. It's easy to love and admire the stubborn female. Damn, what the hell am I going to do?"

"If you love her and want to remain sane, go after her."

"I don't understand. The mating bonds are tight. She shouldn't have been able to leave."

Lissa handed him a goblet of ruby red cranfruit wine. Tamaki's hands curled around the warm goblet as he puzzled over Cimmaron's leaving. Hell, she must really hate him. The thought was sobering. A mate who hated him so much she'd left rather than face him again.

"That's what I'd heard, but possibly it's something to do with her Dlog genes?" Lissa sipped from the steaming goblet. "The two of you are a good match. Go after her. Talk to her. Have you told her how you feel about her?"

"No."

Lissa rolled her eyes. "I thought you were more sensible than most males. You know she wants to fly more than anything. Stopping her flying would be like clipping a Tacon dragon's wings."

"Yeah, I know." Tamaki scowled, a pang of regret lancing through him. He loved Cimmaron, but he'd known all along that this wasn't what she'd wanted. Now he'd driven her away. "That's what I wanted to talk to her about." Tamaki prowled about the room, pausing to pick up a delicate blue urn before setting it back down.

A thump on Lissa's door stopped him mid-step.

"Carry on," Lissa said with another eye roll. "Don't let me stop you. I'll get the door." She glided across the room and disappeared into the passage beyond.

The soft murmur of voices reached him as he trod another circuit of Lissa's room. In the distance, a door thudded, and footsteps approached.

"You have a visitor." Lissa stood aside for someone else to enter the room.

Tamaki froze. "Cimmaron."

"I'll leave the two of you alone," Lissa said, withdrawing and shutting the door before Tamaki had a chance to reply.

He took two steps toward Cimmaron before stopping. Space. She needed time to accept him and their new situation. He opened his mouth to speak then closed it, frightened he'd spook her.

She stood poised just inside the doorway as if she might bolt. "I tried to leave, to get a job on one of the ships flying out. I wanted to leave, but I couldn't damn well stop thinking about you." Her golden eyes flashed with temper, and she stepped closer, jabbing him in the middle of his chest with her forefinger. "What have you done to me? Why can't I get you out of my head?" Her breasts heaved with indignation beneath her brown tunic. "Why?"

Tamaki's heartbeat stuttered on seeing her pain, hearing it in her voice. He loved her. Wasn't that worth something? He hadn't told her. Telling her might help. Another realization crept into his mind. The pain in his chest had faded the *microt* she'd stepped into the room. A part of him wanted to smile even though so much rode on how he presented his case to her. Right now, it was difficult. All he wanted to do was touch her and physically demonstrate his love and desire. He drew in a sharp breath, knowing he needed to wait, that patience would be worth the effort.

A ripple of nerves closed his throat. Tamaki coughed and swallowed, trying to dislodge the tension. "Cimmaron, I didn't mean for this to happen." But he wasn't sorry either. Not the time to admit his lack of regret.

"But you didn't stop it." Tears coated her voice, and her golden eyes looked suspiciously damp.

"I'm an innocent victim too. Do you think I planned on this? I could lose my job for breaking the fraternization rule."

A stricken expression crossed her face. She blinked rapidly. "All I ever wanted to do was fly ships. When I was an underling, I used to watch the dragons glide on the airwaves. I wanted to do the same thing. Fly and explore space."

His mate's misery brought another lump to his throat. Aching to comfort her, he stepped closer and drew her tense body into his arms. For an instant, she remained stiff, then a wispy sigh sounded, and she relaxed against his chest. She trembled, but it felt so right to have her in his arms.

Perfect.

His hands tightened on her shoulders. Then his body reacted to her proximity. His cock pulled tight. *Not now. Wrong time. Wrong place.* He pulled up cold images inside his mind, but it was difficult to remain impassive when the warmth of his mate filled his arms.

Yet again, he cleared his throat. "You can still fly, Cimmaron." Dammit, his plan had to work. He held his breath, waiting for her reaction.

She yanked away from him, aware she'd succumbed to the magical power he seemed to hold over her again. And the blasted aches and pains that had assailed her at the spaceport had all disappeared. The only ache she experienced now was a sexual one. Her folds were moist and tender, her body desperate for his possession. She shifted from foot to foot, the brown tunic heavy and burdensome on her sensitive skin.

She summoned up a glare. "How? Tell me how I can fly when I'm trapped on this forsaken planet with you. The captain of the *Intrepid* has probably filed his AWOL report by now. I'm doomed to stay, chained to your side." Bitterness coated her voice even though, logically, she knew Tamaki wasn't entirely to blame for this situation. She hadn't exactly resisted him at the end. As he'd pointed out, he was a victim too. She paused, trying to think. Yet, no matter which way she turned the situation, she couldn't see a solution.

Stranded.

Mated.

Trapped.

She sniffed, trying to regain control of her frazzled thoughts. "I tried to leave, but I couldn't. My body shut down. The pain in my chest became so bad I couldn't stand on my own. Because of *you*."

"I know." Caring laced his words.

Cimmaron snapped her eyes closed on hearing his sympathetic tone. Why couldn't he yell so she could shout back? A suspicious moistness built behind her closed lids. The truth—he really did know. The funny thing was that if she'd been looking for a mate, she would have loved to find Tamaki. He was a good male. Strong. Handsome. Demanding yet fair. The customers liked him, which was why the club was becoming so successful.

He was a male worthy of love. Cimmaron's mind repeated the thought and stuttered over the concept. Was that the new emotion closing up her throat and pulsing through her veins? This burning in her heart? The need to throw herself at him and never leave his side? Was this love? A tinge of fear snapped at her. *Phrull.*

Stranded.

A tear leaked past her closed lids, and she scrubbed it away with the back of her hand.

"I've transmitted a report to my head office." Tamaki closed the gap between them and stroked his fingers across her cheek.

Cimmaron shivered and bit her lip to stop a purr of contentment from erupting. Kissing would feel so much better. He coughed, and she realized she'd drifted into daydreams again. She couldn't seem to concentrate on anything but Tamaki.

"Did you hear me?"

"Yeah, a report. But what about the fraternization rules Rico was spewing about?"

"I decided honesty was best. I told them everything. About the sabotage. About our mating."

Alarm made her heart pump. She cared about Tamaki. He loved his job just as much as she adored flying. "What...what happened?" They couldn't both lose the things they loved.

"Rico takes over management of the club."

"They're firing you! But you built that club up from nothing. Rico said your club is the top earner in this part of the universe." Cimmaron grabbed his shoulders and shook him vigorously. "You can't let them do this. You must fight them!"

"And I take over the management of the club on Vegamont."

"Fight this!" She paused and frowned. "Vegamont? Did you say Vegamont?"

"Yep." A tiny smile played around his lips.

Cimmaron sighed, a pang of acute envy piercing her heart. "You're so lucky. That's the home base for Vegamont Shipping. And the training school for pilots is there. I'd give anything to move to Vegamont and undertake advanced pilot training."

The tiny smile bloomed to a full-out grin. "You're my mate. I thought you'd come with me."

"With you? You'd really take me with you to Vegamont?" A blip of excitement struck her as she searched his face for truth. His expression displayed not a shred of deception. Tamaki meant it. He really meant it. "You would?"

"Of course, I would. You're my mate. You know those pains you had in the chest?"

Cimmaron nodded, unable to squeeze words past the lump of emotion twisting her gut.

"I had chest pains as well, although they didn't sound as acute as the ones you experienced." Tamaki frowned. "Maybe it's something to do with your Dlog genes."

"The pills aren't working as well as they should either. Ever since I...we...had sex."

"Made love, my mate. Made love." Tamaki cupped her face in his hands and kissed her. Their lips clung together, their breath mingling as they tasted each other. His hands slipped beneath the hem of her brown tunic and slid upward until he cupped her breasts. His thumbs rubbed back and forward over her nipples, and a series of pleasant shockwaves traveled straight to her clit. She purred, a rumbling sound deep in her throat, and her skin took on the familiar sparkle of arousal.

Slowly, Tamaki pulled back. He stared down at her, his blue eyes full of emotion. "You're my mate. We haven't known each other for long, but I love you. Where I go, you go." His fingers played across her breasts until she shuddered helplessly.

"Lo...love." *Phrull*, she couldn't seem to string her words together. He grasped her nipple and twisted. "*Phrull*."

"Yeah, scary, huh?" Tamaki gave her nipple a final tweak before removing his hands from beneath her tunic.

"I..." Cimmaron trailed off and looked him straight in the eye. "I never thought I'd say this to any male, but I feel the same way about you. It sort of crept up on me. I thought it was because of the pills, but no other man interested me. Just you."

Tamaki's hands tightened on her shoulders, his fingers digging into her flesh. His face held an air of urgency. "Say it. Give me the words."

"I love you." Cimmaron felt a moment's uncertainty until a brilliant smile lit his face.

"I knew it," he murmured, stroking her face again.

Cimmaron lifted her hand, finally giving in to the need to return his touch. "Um, it's good that we're going to Vegamont, and you have a new job, but what about me? I'm not cut out to be a full-time bartender. I'm at the stage where if one more male hits on me, I'll run amuck. That won't create a good first impression, and I can't be a stay-at-home mate."

Tamaki laughed, his eyes dancing and twinkling. "We can't have that. Did I happen to mention I have a friend at Vegamont Shipping? He hires the pilots. I could put a good word in for you. And we can stop off on Bezant to clear your name with Coalition Shipping."

"I could fly again?" Please don't let him be teasing. She stared at her mate, hope in her heart. "You'd let me fly? I have friends on Viros, which isn't far from Vegamont. Lynx and Shiloh mentioned wanting to expand their freight business."

"You're my mate, Cimmaron, not a possession. That's what I'm trying to tell you. I want your happiness. Flying makes you happy. If my friend doesn't have a job, you could work for your friends, or maybe you could do more advanced training. You have options. From what I've learned about the mating process, once you stop fighting the bonds, the cramps and chest pains will disappear. We'll be able to spend some time apart as long as we intend to get back together again."

"Tamaki!" Happiness blasted through her, and Cimmaron threw herself into his arms and squeezed him tight. She was going to fly again. Captain. She might even manage to gain captain status. She rained kisses on his face and pressed her body to her mate. Tamaki was nothing like her stepfather. That *male* wouldn't even consider letting his mate—her mother—follow a non-traditional path.

Tamaki laughed, the sound rich and full of amusement. "I'm glad you approve. We'll work out a plan later. What say we adjourn this meeting to the bedroom? We could make love without coercion." He paused to press a lingering kiss on her smiling lips before taking her hand and leading her to the closed door. He opened it and halted to steal another kiss.

Cimmaron led him up the stairs to her room. They stepped inside, closing the door after them for privacy. "Were the servicemen able to fix the green room?"

"Yeah. Rico and I have decided to press charges. I don't care how rich the kid's parents are, he needs to take responsibility for his actions."

"Good." She unfastened the toggles on his shirt and pushed the fabric aside to display his muscled chest and part of his family tattoo. Her fingers danced across his skin.

Hers. Her mate.

The passion bubbled up inside, and her eyes moistened again. *Phrull*, tears were not a good look for a pilot. Leaning closer, she nibbled and teased a flat nipple to prominence. An unknown emotion flooded her body, her mind. *Phrull*, she was smiling. Actually smiling. And it was a toothy grin.

Tamaki grinned back as he toed off his boots and removed his boot linings.

Cimmaron shoved the shirt down his arms, and the garment fluttered to the floor. She unfastened his trews and pushed them and his undergarments down his legs until he stood in naked splendor in front of her. Unable to resist, she ran a finger the length of his erection, tracing the bulbous head.

Tamaki groaned. "I can't wait any longer." He yanked sharply on her tunic, the sound of the ripping fabric loud in the silence of her room. "I'll buy you a new one."

"I didn't like that tunic anyway."

He dealt swiftly with her boots, trews, and undergarments until they were both naked. They fell onto the bed in a tangle of limbs, skin on skin. The start of an erotic assault. One of his hands cupped a breast while he parted her legs with his thigh. A moan fell

139

from her lips when he guided his cock between her legs. A rush of moisture trickled from her pussy, easing his way. With one seamless thrust, he filled her.

"Tamaki," she whispered, raising her hips to meet his next thrust. That this male would change his life to make her happy... The emotion welled even more, threatening to make her cry. She would fly again, and once she'd completed her journey, she had a home and welcoming arms. A mate. Tamaki filled a gap she'd never realized she had in her life. Her hands wrapped around his shoulders, and she clung to him.

He invaded her mouth, exploring the inner surfaces of her mouth, timing his flickering tongue with each deep thrust of his cock. Cimmaron gasped, the heat swirling through her veins. She drew his scent deep into her lungs. Intoxicating. Addictive.

Tamaki lifted his head and brushed a kiss across her pursed lips before withdrawing to the tip of his cock and driving deep again. "God, you feel so good." He withdrew again and thrust, hitting her clit at just the right angle. A tiny ripple started slow and gathered momentum until the sensation filled her, filled her heart, filled her very soul. And in that moment, it felt as if something clicked into place.

The Dlog mating! A gasp of surprise escaped her, along with a sense of wonderment. Now that she'd willingly accepted Tamaki, the Dlog mating chains had cemented them together exactly the way her mother and the Dlog elders had told her.

They were doubly mated. Cimmaron smiled. No longer was she alone, drifting without purpose. No longer stranded or resisting Tamaki, she'd come a full circle.

Cimmaron Zhaan was home.

Thank you so much for reading *Stranded & Seduced*. Word-of-mouth is crucial for any author to succeed. If you enjoyed this book, please consider leaving a review—even a few lines would be a big help.

Sign up for my newsletter for the latest news about my upcoming releases, sales, and bonus content (https://shelleymunro.com/newsletter/).

Turn the page for a glimpse of this romance, a sneak preview of *Seized & Seduced*, the next book in the **House of the Cat** series.

Happy reading,
Shelley xx

EXCERPT – SEIZED & SEDUCED

A shrill cry echoed through the arid valley. Unexpected, it set a shudder rippling the length of her body. Jannike Hondros, second-in-command of the *Indefatigable*, came to an abrupt halt, her stomach twisting anxiously even as she grabbed her blaster out of her hip holster and flicked off the safety.

"Tracker lizards." At her side, Ry Coppersmith, captain of the spaceship, confirmed her fears. He edged his petite mate behind him, but despite her size, Camryn O'Sullivan was no pushover.

She neatly sidestepped him, wincing at a repeat head-splitting shriek, closer this time. "What are tracker lizards, and why are they making that infernal noise?"

"Trackers are the best available means of tracking an object or person. They never fail to capture their target. *Never*. The cries mean they're on a scent," Jannike said tersely, eyes scanning the far end of the valley. She'd experienced their tenacity before and hadn't emerged on the winning side.

"Us." Ry glanced at Jannike, and with the ease of a long friendship, they came to a decision without words.

Jannike gave him an imperceptible nod. "We need to split up," she said abruptly, attention on the horizon. She caught the swirl of approaching dust in the distance, maybe four or five clicks. "You need to shift, change your scents."

"But Mogens said shifting might be dangerous." Camryn cupped her slim belly in protest.

"We're going to have to risk it," Ry said without hesitation. "It's either that or capture."

"Capture? What's going on? This sort of thing doesn't happen on Earth. Usually," Camryn added, obviously thinking about her own kidnapping several cycles earlier.

"I'll keep going away from the ship," Jannike said, a lump the size of a rock closing up her throat, making the words gravely. She swallowed dryly, silently cursing both the situation and this god-awful heat from the planet's sun. The dry temperatures sucked the juice from everything, animal and vegetable. "Go." It was surprisingly difficult to force out the order.

Camryn still frowned, not understanding. She squinted at her husband, shifted her attention to Jannike. "But—"

"Change. Now," Ry barked. "Jannike, if you're captured, we'll come for you. We will not give up. That's a pledge."

"Same goes." Secs later, she started running, veering around the pile of rocks and sprinting down the rolling sand hill away from Ry and Camryn. It had to be the cargo ship they'd seen earlier, but why had they set tracker lizards on them?

A thought sprang into her mind, and she stumbled before

regaining her balance. *Grata.* No, it couldn't be *her.* No, that was impossible when Jannike was light years away from her home planet.

Behind her, the baying shrieks of the lizards intensified. Sweat trickled down her forehead, stinging her eyes. She slipped in the shifting sand, arms flailing before she toppled, hitting the ground hard enough to knock the breath from her lungs.

No time to baby herself. She had to move. Faster. She had to give Ry and Camryn time to get to the ship. Otherwise, the entire crew could get sucked into whatever trouble they'd blundered into this day. Her blue tunic clung like a lover. A skin wet from sweat. The dry rocks in her throat closed her windpipe. She panted, a painful wheeze. Gods, she had to keep going. She twisted, rolled, and pushed to her feet. She lurched her first steps, only her fitness and determination propelling her forward.

Concentrate on running. Forget the trackers. Don't think about the past.

The landscape stretched endlessly in front of her—one big, inhospitable sandpit. Overhead, the planet's sun beat down, frying everything in its path. And still she kept trying to run. One foot in front of the other, leading the trackers farther away from the *Indy.* Faster. Faster. The *Indy's* crew were her friends, her family, and she'd do anything to keep them safe.

Determination gave her a burst of speed, but a glance over her shoulder told her the trackers had dramatically closed the distance between them. Their brown-blue bodies glinted in the bright light, strangely beautiful despite their ferocity. Their baying cries filled her head, lent panic to her adrenaline-fueled flight. She rounded a corner and came to an abrupt halt. A box canyon. The wall of rock stretched into the distance as far as she could see.

Trapped.

Nowhere to go.

Slowly, chest rising and falling in uneven gasps, she turned to face the four snapping trackers. Their bulging eyes blinked slowly, their wicked teeth white against the brown-blue of their skin. Their stubby tails shifted lazily from side to side, strong muscles in their haunches poised to spring should she attempt a sudden move. She edged along the rock wall, and they moved with her. She'd heard their bite was nasty, and some people were highly allergic to their saliva.

But she refused to go without a fight. She reached for a handhold on the rock wall, digging her fingertips, attempted to lever her body upward.

"Ho, my beauties. What have you caught me today?" The mountain of a man rode up on a cyber-beest—a combination of machine and cheetahbeest by the look of the tawny coat and spots. The cyber-beest snorted, pawing at the ground, restive under the firm restraint. The large rider wore a tight, light gray suit, shaped to his body. The man was all muscle with no fat. With his left hand, he controlled the cyber-beest while his right rested lightly on a coiled whip.

Jannike glanced left, speared a look right. A tracker bite or the nip of Mountain Man's whip. Both would hurt.

"You won't escape," Mountain Man said with almost a kind smile. But the smile didn't reach his wintry-blue eyes, and she knew, deep in her gut, that he wouldn't hesitate to do whatever he needed to do to capture her. *Fukk, her past had come back to bite her in the bum. There was no other explanation.* "Why are you chasing me?"

"Why did you run?" the man countered.

Grab your copy of **Seized & Seduced** today.
(https://shelleymunro.com/books/seized-seduced/)

ABOUT SHELLEY

USA Today bestselling author Shelley Munro lives in Auckland, the City of Sails, with her husband and a cheeky Jack Russell/mystery breed dog.

Typical New Zealanders, Shelley and her husband left home for their big OE soon after they married (translation of New Zealand speak - big overseas experience). A twelve-month-long adventure lengthened to six years of roaming the world. Enduring memories include being almost sat on by a mountain gorilla in Rwanda, lazing on white sandy beaches in India, whale watching in Alaska, searching for leprechauns in Ireland, and dealing with ghosts in an English pub.

While travel is still a big attraction, these days Shelley is most likely found in front of her computer following another love - that of writing stories of contemporary and paranormal romance and adventure. Other interests include watching rugby (strictly for research purposes), cycling, playing croquet and the ukelele, and curling up with an enjoyable book.

Visit Shelley at her Website
https://shelleymunro.com

Join Shelley's Newsletter
https://shelleymunro.com/newsletter

ALSO BY SHELLEY

Middlemarch Shifters
My Scarlet Woman
My Younger Lover
My Peeping Tom
My Assassin
My Estranged Lover
My Feline Protector
My Determined Suitor
My Cat Burglar
My Stray Cat
My Second Chance
My Plan B
My Cat Nap
My Romantic Tangle
My Blue Lady
My Twin Trouble
My Precious Gift

Middlemarch Gathering
My Highland Mate
My Highland Fling
My Elusive Mate
My Valiant Princess
My Highland Wedding
My Highland Billionaire

House of the Cat
Captured & Seduced
Claimed & Seduced
Merry & Seduced
Stranded & Seduced
Seized & Seduced
Hunted & Seduced
Festive & Seduced
Betrayed & Seduced
Enticed & Seduced

Dragon Investigators
Blue Moon Dragon
Blood Moon Dragon
Black Moon Dragon
Snow Moon Dragon

Dragon Isles
Liza
Cherry
Rena
Sasha

www.ingramcontent.com/pod-product-compliance
Lightning Source LLC
Chambersburg PA
CBHW050820180626
46814CB00004B/1379